A

Yreka:
10-15-01
Mt.Shasta:

Etna:

Weed:
1-23-02
Tulelake:
3-26-02
Dunsmuir:
6-25-02
Yreka:

THANKSGIVING

THANKSGIVING

—⁂—

Michael Dibdin

||
35

PANTHEON BOOKS NEW YORK

Pantheon Books and colophon are registered trademarks
of Random House, Inc.

Library of Congress Cataloging-in-Publication Data

Dibdin, Michael.
Thanksgiving / Michael Dibdin.
p. cm.
ISBN 0-375-42098-3
1. British—Nevada—Fiction. 2. Middle aged men—Fiction. 3. Midlife
crisis—Fiction. 4. Journalists—Fiction. 5. Remarriage—Fiction.
6. Widowers—Fiction. 7. Nevada—Fiction. I. Title.

PR6054.I26 T48 2001   823'.914—dc21   00-058892

www.pantheonbooks.com

Printed in the United States of America

First American Edition

2 4 6 8 9 7 5 3 1

Griefe lurkes in secret angles of the heart.

JOHN MARSTON, *Antonio's Revenge*

FOR KATHERINE

LUCY IN THE SKY

At night in the desert you can see for ever, which is where Lucy first appears. Taking this old road, a thin red line on the Rand McNally map, seemed a fun prospect at the time, but it isn't working out that way. So far from there being more to see – after dark on a cold October evening? – there is, if anything, less.

Back on the new highway, there'd at least be some other traffic to keep you company. But this road's no longer travelled, and you can see why. The untended surface has gone to pieces, patched and potholed, ribbed from the summer heat and infiltrated by a scree of sand blown in from either side, depending on the vagaries of the wind. At the speed you need to make sense of this invisible land-scape, you could easily end up spinning out and flipping over if you didn't constantly keep alert. Which isn't easy, hour after hour, with nothing to do but scan the wedge of blacktop which the car drives before it.

So when light appears on the horizon dead ahead, it

immediately assumes an importance out of all proportion to its actual magnitude. Just a distant glow is all. A brush fire, it might be, if anything grew out here. An oncoming vehicle, but it would be the first so far. Maybe a town, if there were any. It could be anything, quite frankly. Or nothing.

Problems with the surface aside, the rental car handles like a dream. On Highway 93 you could have set the cruise control to around a hundred and then snuggled down in the heated, ergonomically adjustable seat, finger-tipping the power steering while the radio warbled sweet nothings and the big eighteen-wheelers ate your dust. But you have to work at this bitch of a road. Let one of those craters in the surface catch you fumbling and you'd be belly up in the scrub before you could spit. As for music, forget it. Nothing grows in this wilderness of static but ghostly gibberish.

Sometime later, you realize that the light source up ahead has taken on a recognizable form. Human, to be precise. You can't believe your eyes at first, but there comes a time when you have to. Not long afterwards, it becomes apparent that the luminoid is sexed as well, her charms displayed in varying shades of red, the intensity reflecting the erogenous rating of the zone in question, while a continual alternation of three static poses creates an illusion of mobility. At once grandly proportioned and intimately detailed, the female figure shimmers and pulses in the swirling air. All her parts are cosmic. She consumes acres of sky, an erotic constellation.

Once past a certain point the pattern starts to disintegrate again, rapidly losing shape and sense as you close in on it. Under that mass of meaningless lights, you now make out the familiar contours of a gas station with garage and diner attached. The concrete forecourt is cracked and crazed, the office roofless and gutted, the eatery boarded up. In every corner, the wind is busily hoarding dirt. The entire scene is bathed in the suffused light of countless red and white bulbs mounted in apparently random profusion on a painted hoarding attached to a metal tower some fifty feet high, heavily rusted and swaying alarmingly in the wind that moans as the structure troubles for an instant its passage through the enormous darkness.

I opened the glove compartment and slipped the loaded revolver into my coat pocket, feeling faintly ridiculous. By the shifting light cast by the bulbs overhead, I made out a figure walking towards me across the forecourt.

'Gas?' he called out. 'You'll need to pull over to the pump.'

Lucy had apparently taken the family photographs, so while she never appeared, Darryl Bob Allen was in almost every one. The burly physique, the bristling beard, the long hair tied back in a ponytail, the affectless gaze. He always looked slightly ill at ease, as though a photograph might find out the flaw he hid in movement in real life.

She'd told me about a prenatal clinic they'd attended, before Claire was born, where she was thinking about each couple: 'He did it with her.' Her husband's patriarchal pose in those photos was the same. The notional subject, baby Claire or wee Frank, was duly dandled and presented, but their father's expression was one of detached, impersonal pride, as though to say 'I stuck it in her and shot my wad, and here's the living proof.'

I got out of the car.

'Hi. I'm Anthony.'

He looked away to one side.

'Oh, right. You're real late. I'd just about given up on you.'

Lucy had always rated charm and a good voice. Unsurprisingly, Darryl Bob turned out to have both.

I shrugged apologetically.

'It took longer than I counted on. I thought all the maps in the road atlas were the same, but it turns out Nevada is half the scale of the ones I've used before. I'd figured on about two hours, but it ended up taking more than twice that.'

I didn't mention the time I'd spent getting used to aiming and firing the revolver.

'Yeah, well, welcome to America. About the only thing the several states have in common is you have to drive on the right. Plus frankly there ain't that much to put on a map out here. It's wall-to-wall sweet fuck all, basically.'

I pointed up at the mast with its array of coloured bulbs flicking on and off.

'Except for this.'

He smiled in a diffident, boyish way. I'd never imagined this side to him. In those photographs he was always scowling purposefully at the camera. It occurred to me for the first time that he maybe just didn't like being photographed.

'Oh, that's a little private project. Got it from a beach resort down in La Jolla. There used to be a neon display in the centre with the name of the place, just below her breasts, but I took that off. Kind of liked it more abstract, know what I mean?'

'It's certainly eye-catching. Especially out here in the middle of nowhere.'

'There's a ton more. Want to see?'

He seemed genuinely eager. We walked over to the concrete garage, opened the door and turned on a light. The entire space inside was filled with huge signs, stacked one against the other. In the corner there was a sink and photographic equipment.

'I've got others out back. One thing about living here, you can just leave stuff lying outside, like those planes the Air Force stores round here. I was planning to mount them all, one time. Wire them up, create a kind of neon theme park. Thought it might get some touristic interest going out here. I mean, this is like a lost folk art, you know?'

All the while he was taking stock of me, in a surreptitious way. In the days when Allen still lived close to us, he'd used to drop by occasionally to take the children out for some Disneyland Dad treat, but Lucy had tactfully arranged matters so that we never met. He'd never seen a photograph of me, of course, and was naturally curious to see what his successor looked like.

'These must have cost a fortune,' I remarked.

Lucy had made a big point of the fact that Allen had never paid her a dime in child support, yet he had apparently been making grand plans for leisure attractions in the middle of the desert.

'They're kind of pricey now, but I was ahead of the curve. People used to see them as scrap. Junk, even. You could pick them up for next to nothing.'

'And that?' I asked, gesturing at the photographic equipment.

Allen smiled in an odd, knowing way.

'Oh, that's another hobby of mine.'

I thought of all those amateurish snapshots in the family album, ill-composed and badly exposed, often with a finger creeping over the lens. Those were the ones I had seen, the ones which Lucy had taken. If photography was one of Allen's interests, why hadn't he taken any pictures?

'Yeah, I used to be heavy into photography,' he added, closing up the shed. 'Did it for a living, one time. Plus some of the stuff I took you couldn't exactly take to the drugstore to get developed.'

'How do you mean?'

'I mean it might have got me arrested. Anyway, the

quality of that commercial stuff is shit, and you can't crop and home in the way you can if you do it yourself. Saves money, too.'

'Talking of that, you have this on all the time?' I asked, pointing up at the mast swaying in the gusts of wind sweeping in out of the night.

'Twenty-four hours a day. This is a gas station. We never close. We lose a little bit on every sale, but we make up for it in volume.'

'Your light bill must be pretty steep.'

'Comes free. Up on top there's a wind vane I cannibalized from a heating system upgrade. It's hooked up to a generator back of my trailer. As long as the wind blows, the current flows. The tower came from an AM radio station that went out of business. Only cost a couple of hundred bucks, those guys just wanted it out of there. I dismantled it, trucked it out here and put it back up again.'

'Big job.'

'Luce always said I was good with my hands.'

He laughed.

'But then she told you the same thing, didn't she?'

'I'm hopeless as a handyman. If I've got a little problem, I write a little cheque. And how can you possibly know what Lucy told me?'

'I just do. When it comes to Luce, I've been there, done that. Got the whole situation taped, so to speak.'

With a broad smile, he jerked his head to one side.

'Let's go.'

He strode off across the forecourt. I followed, my hand in my right pocket to disguise the sagging bulge on that side. I'd bought the revolver that afternoon at a gun show I stumbled into when I took a wrong turning leaving the airport terminal and found myself in one of the halls of a convention centre. The vast impersonal space was lined with home-made stalls covered in lengths of cloth or plastic and decorated with handwritten signs. The event might easily have been an antique market or a used book fair, but these folks were selling weapons. Just about every conceivable form of firearm was on display. I didn't see any tanks or rocket launchers, but I had no doubt that they were available to special order. I did see one old geezer carrying an automatic assault rifle over his shoulder. The paper flag stuck into the barrel read: 'Only $400. Barely used.'

I'd bought the revolver on impulse from a morose, tubby man who said he went by 'Lefty'. I gave him a story about needing to defend my home from the scum who were running around these days. He nodded in a sympathetic but slightly bored way. He didn't care what I was going to do with the gun any more than a car salesman cares where you plan to drive. All Lefty wanted to do was make a sale. He proceeded to describe the technical virtues and drawbacks of the various models he had on sale. As he talked me through each one, he picked it up and put it in my hand. It was an odd feeling. I realized that I had never before touched something which was solely and specifically designed to kill.

Once round the corner of the abandoned gas station, the wind was harsh and relentless. Lights were showing in an aluminium trailer mounted on concrete blocks. Darryl Bob Allen leapt up a set of three steps and opened the door.

'Come on in,' he said.

The interior of the trailer seemed cramped but cosy. The walls had been lined with some sort of wood facing, the floor was carpeted. Stacks of shelving and cupboards to either side left a narrow passageway which eventually opened into a small living area with a beaten-up leather sofa, a swivel chair, a stereo and a TV. In the centre stood a cast-iron woodstove with a galvanized chimney pipe running up to the roof. The air was warm and pleasantly scented with woodsmoke. A thirties-style wooden standard lamp with a pleated cloth shade stood in the corner, the light wavering and flickering like the bulbs on the sign outside.

'How 'bout a little music?'

Without waiting for an answer, Allen pushed a button on the tape deck.

I can see, right out my window,
Walking down the street, my girl,
With another guy.
His arms around her like it used to be with me.
Oh, it makes me want to die.

He made a few dance-like steps in time with the music. He clearly danced well, with both grace and power. Another thing Lucy had implied in an unguarded moment was that her ex-husband had been both energetic and eager to please in bed.

'What you think?' he asked.

He was referring to the music, or maybe his stereo rig, but I chose to misunderstand.

'You dance really well.'

'Not as good as Luce,' he said, sitting down in the swivel chair. 'Man, she was good. Put her whole body into it, but at the same time she was always in perfect control. Know what I mean? You can tell when a woman's good, and believe me, she was good.'

He laughed.

'She used to complain sometimes, next morning, that her feet hurt. I said to her, your *feet*? You like to dance? You ever dance with her?'

> *Here it comes.*
> *Oh here it comes.*
> *Yeah here it comes.*
> *Here comes the night.*

Allen turned the tape off abruptly and pushed the rewind button. While the tape was whirring away, he strode off into the darkness at the far end of the trailer, returning with a quart jug of Canadian whiskey and two glasses. The tape clacked to a stop. He stuck it in its box and seemed about to replace it on the shelving stacked with other cassette and VCR tapes. Then he seemed to change his mind and laid it on the table.

'Want a drink?' he asked.

'No thanks. I have to drive later.'

'You're heading back tonight? That's a long way. Hell, I can put you up here. The sofa turns into a bed, kind of.'

Still standing, Allen poured a glass for himself. He was swaying slightly, and I realized that he was drunk. He'd probably started early, expecting me to arrive hours ago. So much the better. It would make things easier, when the time came.

'Nice place you've made here,' I remarked conversationally.

'It's all right. I've got my tapes, my videos, my photography.'

He smiled in a way I couldn't interpret.

'My memories.'

'No books, though.'

'I have *the* book. Only one I need.'

Oh, so he was one of those, I thought. Lucy hadn't told me about this aspect of his personality. Or maybe he'd found Christ after she dumped him.

He pointed out a shelf of about twenty identical, tall, narrow volumes bound in black.

'The *Encyclopaedia Britannica*,' he declaimed in a parody of an English accent. 'The 1911 edition, complete in twenty-eight volumes, not counting the index and maps. I'm about three-quarters of the way through, so far. Reading about the poet Ovid in a volume entitled "Ode to Pay". Ovid never wrote a poem called that, as far as they know, and those guys knew everything, but I think it could have been a big hit. Sort of Robert W. Service bar-room ballad stuff. Strong subject. Like I always say, the two oldest lies are "Your cheque's in the mail" and "I promise I won't come in your mouth." You a reader?'

'Must have cost a fair amount, that set.'

'I got it for fifty dollars. The library had a sale. Wanted all new stuff, didn't know what it was worth. I had to make a trip through Carson anyway, get wood for the stove. I go once a year, up into the National Forest other side of Lake Tahoe. Find a couple of fallers, cut them to length with a chainsaw and winch them on to the half-ton. Back here I split and stack 'em. Lasts me all through the winter.'

'Isn't that illegal?'

'Never got caught yet. There's not a lot of law out here, and what there is is spread awful thin. So go ahead and have as much booze as you want. You'll never get popped for DWI round here.'

He sat back down again, crossed his legs and stared at me directly for what I realized then was the first time. Every eye-contact earlier had been brief, oblique and teasing.

This was confrontational. The warm-up was over and the game was about to begin.

'So, you said you wanted to talk about the kids. How are the little charmers, anyway? It's kind of hard to keep in touch, having to go out to some bar to phone and all. Last I heard Claire's husband ran off with another woman leaving her holding the kid, what's his name?'

'Daniel.'

'But Frank seems to be doing pretty good. Guy takes after me, always did. He'll be okay.'

He slurped some whiskey and looked at me.

'So your point is, Tone? Or should I call you Tony? We all know how toney you Brits are. Like to think you are, anyway. No, Tone sounds right to me. Tone it is.'

'Talking about what sounds right, do you want to drop the cornball idiom? "Doing pretty good", and all the rest of it. You've got a degree from UC Berkeley, Lucy told me. Don't try playing the hick with me.'

'Why, I'm sorry. I guess living out here with the kind of people who live out here, you sort of adapt to the way they talk.'

He stood up and stepped towards me. At that moment, the light dimmed for a moment.

'The wind,' Allen explained, looming above me. 'When it drops, the power goes out. Here, let me take your coat. It's awful hot in here. Awfully hot, I mean. Frightfully hot. Dreadfully hot. Appallingly hot. And all that rot.'

'No, thanks.'

'Believe me, you'd be better off without it. You're start-ing to sweat.'

'I'm fine.'

He paused there a moment, then returned to his chair.

'Actually, just for the record, I never did go to college. Fact is I was what you might call a high-school drop-out.'

'That's not what Lucy told me,' I said as the light surged back.

'Well, that makes sense, because it's not what I told her. But I was trying to get into her pants, you see, and the first rule of successful salesmanship is "Don't knock the mer-chandise." If the customer likes what she sees, and I have to tell you she did, then your job as a salesman is to vali-date her decision. Reassure her that she's made the right choice. Which I did, with maybe a little hyperbole built in. You ever been to the Hyperbowl, Tone? It's kind of like the Superbowl, only more so.'

'Can we get back to the point?'

'Which is?'

'The will.'

'What will?'

'I've been talking to the children about how we should manage the estate.'

'Luce made a will? Well, I'll be. Never thought she'd have gotten around to it. She left everything to the kids, I guess.'

'"Everything" is basically the house. They each get a third, I get the rest.'

'Oh, really? You did all right, then. That place must be worth close to quarter of a million these days. It was a total fixer-upper when we bought it, but the neighbourhood demographic's changed some since then.'

Lucy and I had had the house valued a few months earlier. The realtor said we should list it at two-seventy and expect to sell for at least two-fifty.

'You seem very well informed,' I replied.

'Real estate's another little hobby of mine. Anyway, I notice I don't get a cent, so what's all this to do with me?'

'What it's got to do with you is that Claire, Frank and I have to decide whether or not to sell up and cash in now – which would of course mean me moving – or wait a while. A factor in that equation is knowing what expectations if any they have from you.'

'How do you mean, expectations?'

'What provisions have you made for your children in *your* will?'

Darryl Bob Allen stretched lazily.

'Well, tell you the truth I haven't actually got around to making out a will just yet. I'm planning on hanging in here a while yet.'

'Of course. That's what we all plan on. But the fact is you could die any time. Even tonight. You never know.'

'You mean a person?'

'What person?'

'A person never knows? Or I, me, myself, specifically don't know?'

'I'm just trying to work out what's the deal for the kids. I'm sure we both want the best for them, Darryl.'

'Oh, sure.'

He sighed and waved his hand around.

'Well, this is basically all I've got. If they want it, they're welcome to it. I mean, there's no one else in the picture. They'll get it anyway, will or no will.'

'You have no other dependants?'

He shook his head, a single decisive swipe which reminded me uncannily of Lucy. She must have copied it from him, I realized, or he from her.

'So that's it?' he asked.

'What's what?'

'You came all the way down here for that? Hell, we could have done that when I called you from town.'

He refilled his glass.

'But that's not really why you came, is it?'

'Why else?'

He beamed at me through his lumberjack beard.

'You came to see me!'

'Why would I do that?'

'Well, I'm just guessing here, admittedly. But you've just lost your wife, right? I lost her too, but that was a while ago. I've had time to get used to it. Plus I had her for longer in the first place, and in better shape. But for you the grief is still fresh, like they say, and you'd only known her for a few years. So the bit of her you knew was like the tip of the iceberg, and now the iceberg's sunk. You know that old joke? "*Titanic* Collides With Iceberg. Iceberg Undamaged." Where was I?'

'You were asking why I came down here in person. Well, one reason was just to get away. The past few weeks have been quite intense.'

'I imagine. Listen, I'm real sorry I couldn't make the funeral.'

'There was no funeral. You need a body for that.'

'Well, the service or whatever. But I sort of felt maybe it wouldn't be right.'

'Very tactful of you.'

'And then of course there was the money angle. I sell a little gas here. Only station for eighty miles in one direction, sixty-two in the other. Problem is, there's hardly any traffic on this road. Then once in a while I do some construction work down in Vegas. Man, you should see that place! You can stand there and watch it grow. Take a lunch break and there's a whole new sub-development.'

Once again the lights died quietly, then came back. Allen leant forward and poured some whiskey into the other glass.

'Come on, Tone,' he said. 'Don't let me drink alone

here. Listen, you're welcome to sleep on the sofa. I really mean that. On one condition, and that's that you're not a happy breakfaster. I myself always need a couple of hours to remember who the hell I am, so don't count on any scintillating table-talk. But I'll brew a pot of coffee and pack you on your way in broad daylight, instead of you squinting at some unmarked road for hours on end. Anyway, you want to talk. I know you do.'

'Talk about what?'

'About Luce, of course. Admit it, you're curious. That's okay. You'd have to be crazy not to be curious. Oh, it was fine while she was still alive, although I bet even then you must have had the occasional nagging question about this or that. But it didn't matter then. She was here, you were a couple, you hit the sack together every night. Who cared what happened before you met? That was all history.'

He reached a box of cigars down from a shelf, stuck one between his lips and lit it with a splinter of wood from the stove.

'But now *she's* history,' he went on, exhaling a cloud of blueish smoke. 'Your marriage is history, just like mine. The only difference is that if we're talking history, Luce and I had more and better. And you're bound to be curious about that. Who wouldn't be?'

He beamed at me again.

'So go ahead. Slake that curiosity. Ask away. I promise to answer freely and frankly to the best of my ability.'

I shifted slightly to move the angular bulk of the revolver off my hip, where it was beginning to ache.

'Still shy?' said Allen. 'Or "in denial", like they say these days. Okay, I understand. Look, how about if I kick this one off? For example, I imagine you're probably wondering how we met.'

Indeed. I had occasionally tried to get Lucy to talk about her time with Darryl Bob, but she almost always shied away from the topic. 'I hate the past,' she'd say.

'Well, it was at a party. Nothing very original, I'm afraid. I was working as a freelance photographer at the time, but I was also drummer in a rock band in the evenings. We used to get some good people stopping by. I can remember jamming with a bunch of guys who were big names even then, and legends now. Garcia, Crosby, Cipollina . . . I always think John was underestimated as a guitarist.

'Anyway, what with that and the photography, I got invited to a lot of parties, and one night at some house in the Panhandle, there she was. This was, what? Early seventies? I had a nice little three-way deal going at the time. This one little skinny blonde number, and then a real mamma, gallons of oomph, tits bigger than your head, roll-'em-in-flour-and-see-where-the-wet-spot-is type, know what I mean? So anyway, what with Liz and Deb I was getting laid pretty good, but I could tell right away that Luce was something special. Great body, but acted like she didn't know it. We got dancing. Luce always loved to dance. You ever dance with her? Oh, I already asked that. Anyway, one thing led to another and we ended up back at her place. She had a nice little room in a funky old Victorian on Haight, just around the corner from the Free Clinic. Must be worth over a million now.'

He smiled.

'What I remember best about it is the way she took her clothes off. A lot of chicks were self-conscious about that part, even back then. They either wanted to be undressed during a scuffle on the sofa, or do a kind of amateur strip-tease routine, or else go into the bathroom and reappear magically naked. Luce just stood there and took off her clothes, completely casual and matter-of-fact, just like she was alone. Which just made it worse. I just about died there and then. No, actually I just about burst into tears. Dumb, huh? I mean, I'd been around the block a few times. I must have had forty or fifty women by then. Like they say, who's counting? But when I saw Luce standing there nude, I felt humbled. I really did. Like when you hear some great piece of music or something. I thought, I don't deserve this.'

He laughed.

'Then I thought, but hey, since it's come my way I guess I'll grab myself a piece of it anyway.'

He looked at me.

'You know the real problem with fucking? It's not the Darwinian angle. You know, the peak experience that turns out to be a flashy sales pitch by your genes, like the casinos sending a private plane down to wherever to lure some high roller back to the tables and take him for everything he's worth. That's kind of depressing, once you get it, but it's just a mind thing. You can work around that one. No, what always bugged me about the whole thing is you can't look at them and fuck them at the same time. And believe me, Luce was worth looking at, back then. But of course next thing you're squished up together playing hide the salami and frankly it could be anyone down there. I mean you get the occasional glimpse, of course, depending on the position and so forth, but it's tough to really get the whole action in perspective, know what I mean? That's one reason I got interested in the picture angle. Still sure you don't want to take your coat off, Tone? No? Suit yourself, but I have to say you're sweating like a pig. Kind of a strange expression, when you think about it. I've never seen a pig sweat. I'm not even sure they do sweat. Except maybe at the slaughterhouse.'

During the drive, I had turned off the highway on to a dirt track which led up into a range of low, rounded bluffs, ending at a disused mine of some sort. There I took a rest break and got in some target practice, firing at an array of cereal boxes I'd picked up at a convenience store on the outskirts of the city. Lefty had told me that if that hypothetical intruder entered my home, the upper chest area was the place to go for. I measured a twenty-ounce Cheerios box against my own chest. It seemed about right.

After about an hour, and a pack and a half of cartridges, I'd managed to demolish all but one of the boxes, each producing a satisfying shower of honey-coated wheat cereal all over the surrounding rock. By then the revolver, which had initially shocked me with its alien power, had settled down to become an extension of my arm, a hardened and potentially lethal prosthesis. I had no intention of killing Darryl Bob Allen, but I knew that this artificial limb wouldn't have the slightest compunction about doing so.

'What do you mean by the picture angle?' I said.

'Photos. Snapshots. Et cetera. Some even from back when we got together.'

He grinned.

'But of course a toney guy like you wouldn't be interested in that sort of thing, would you, Tone? You were interested in Miss Lucy as a person, right? Well, good for you. Dull work, but someone's got to do it.'

'Where did you get them?'

'Get what?'

'The photographs.'

'Ah, the *photographs*,' he said in his fake English accent. 'Same as my phonograph over there, old chap. I took them from our house. This was a year or so before you moved in. After she told me it was all over and I had to go, blah-di-blah, I actually ended up staying on there another few months. I had nowhere else to go, you see, being as luck would have it temporarily unemployed at that particular point in time. She tell you that?'

'Of course.'

'You said that a little too quickly, Tone. Not your style, I think. And not hers, either. To tell you, I mean. Luce would have been too kind to tell you a thing like that, knowing how it might hurt you. Just as she was too kind to chuck the father of her children out on the streets. So I ended up living there till a friend of hers found me a job at the university. Yep, that philosophy degree finally paid off after all. Actually the position was as one of the janitors, but hey, the pay was good and I took it philosophically. Anyway, meanwhile I carried right on living with her in that house you know so well, like nothing had really changed. We even slept in the same bed. Had to, you see. The kids had the other rooms.'

There was a lengthy silence.

'Now I know what you're thinking,' Allen continued, 'except you're too polite to ask. At least, I think I know. Let me have a shot at it anyway. I'd be prepared to place a modest bet that what you're thinking is, *Did they fuck?*'

He took a long draw on his cigar and washed the smoke down with some more whiskey.

'Well, the answer is in the affirmative. Luce didn't want to, but when push came to shove she didn't say no. Or at any rate, not real convincingly. She was too hot to last even one month without some pussy action, never mind three. But she must have made a deal with herself. She'd let me fuck her, but she wasn't going to come. Or at least, she wasn't going to let me know I'd made her come.'

He laughed, slapping his hands together.

'And you know what? Those last months of our marriage was the best sex I ever had in my whole goddamn life. Imagine fucking this hot babe's brains out, knowing all the time that she's fighting her own orgasm. We're talking truly mind-blowing stuff here.'

He poured himself more whiskey and pushed the other glass towards me.

'Come on, Tone, take your medicine like a good boy. You're going to need it before I get through.'

'Through with what?'

'Satisfying what killed the cat. I mean, let's get real. We both have an agenda here. I have my memories, you have a gun.'

I recrossed my legs involuntarily, shielding the right side of my body.

'A gun? What are you talking about?'

'Well, maybe you're just glad to see me.'

He laughed again.

'Anyway, before I finally had to leave and get an apartment of my own, I had lots of time to go through our photo collection and pull out the ones I wanted. Luce was at work all day and the kids were at school, so I had the run of the house. Sure you don't want to see them? The prints haven't worn that well, the ones I wasn't able to find the negs for, but they'll still give you an idea.'

He stood up, tossing his cigar butt into the stove.

'Let's see, where did I put those things? This place used to be a total mess, but I knew exactly where everything was. Then I got one of my manic spells a while back and decided to tidy up. Now I can't find jack shit. Some of those early ones are really something. Luce used to make most of her clothes, to save money, and I have to say she was pretty damn good. She knew how to dress herself to cause a stir without causing a riot, you know? When she went out alone, she always dressed defensively. Had to, to avoid unwanted attention on the streets. But when she was with me she could loosen up a little, go without a bra and let it all hang loose. Even after feeding Claire her tits were still as perky as ever. Frank took them down another notch or two, but back then I used to get a real rush walking down the street with her, my arms around her, like Van the Man says, knowing that every guy around was getting a hard-on just looking at her. That ever happen to you?'

He looked at me.

'What's the matter, Tone? You don't say nothing. You're not inhibited, are you? The stereotypical uptight Brit? We're just a couple of guys here. We can talk freely.'

'I'll speak my piece later.'

'Or your piece will speak for you. You're not planning to shoot me, are you?'

'Don't be ridiculous.'

'Pardon my asking. Just a thought that occurred to me. You know how we no-class Americans can't help blabbing out anything that crosses our minds. Where were we? I'm losing my grip. Time for another hit.'

He sat down and gulped some more whiskey.

'Right, those photos. And that's not all. I was kind of unhappy about Luce kicking me out, tell you the truth. In fact I was seriously pissed off. So to get even, I decided to sort of keep an eye on her for a while, see what transpired. And that's how I come to have the tapes of her and Scott.'

He paused.

'You know about Scott?'

'I think she mentioned the name.'

'What did she say?'

'I don't remember.'

'Forgive me, I'm curious to know how she pitched it.'

'She said something about him being a co-worker and that they'd gone to Japan together on some sales trip.'

'Did she tell you that they'd done the deed? That's what she would have said, I'll bet. "Done the deed." She loved those corny old expressions.'

He looked at me.

'She didn't? Well, I don't blame her. Personally, I think

it was a mite reckless of her to mention Scott at all. Don't scare the new horse, would have been my advice. So obviously she didn't tell you what happened once they got back. She didn't tell me either, of course, but I found out just the same because I was stalking her at the time, like I said. And I have to tell you that once Scott and Luce got back from that sales trip to Tokyo they proceeded to do the very same deed at least a dozen times more back in town. It sounds dumb, but that kind of shocked me. I mean, I didn't expect Luce to remain celibate, but I somehow didn't expect to be replaced so soon. Although I have to say that given what she was after, she made a pretty good choice. This Scott was a real studly guy, some kind of work-out fanatic, one of those abs-of-steel types. He liked to get her to walk on his stomach. Wish I'd been able to have her do that. She must have looked pretty good from that angle.'

'How do you know all this?'

He frowned at me.

'Are you paying attention? I told you. I taped them at it. Well, some of it, anyway. But I've got pretty lengthy extracts from eight sessions. They used a motel, you see. Luce had the kids at home and Scott had a wife. And since they had no reason to suppose that anyone suspected them, they always used the same motel. So I checked out the facility in question, and figured out that whatever the room number, the bed was always on the left-hand side of the unit. After that, it was just a question of following Luce down there, seeing which room she went into, and then trying for the one next to it. "107 free? I'll take that." Sometimes it was, sometimes it wasn't. Then a microphone embedded in a suction cup sticker attached to the party wall, and I got to record the whole party. The sound quality isn't that great, compared with what I got up to later, but it's okay. They were mostly quite loud, anyway. You can surely make out what was going on.'

He stood up unsteadily.

'Want to hear one? March eighteenth is my favourite. That's right before Scott's wife found out what was going on and the shit hit the fan. The interesting thing is that you can kind of sense, unless this is just me, that Luce already knew that something was up. She was always good at that, sort of premonition stuff. Anyway, there's an edge of desperation there that's lacking in the earlier tapes, when she was just thinking of the moment. The down side is there's also a lot of talk about how she feels guilty and doesn't want to wreck his marriage and all that, but that just makes the action scenes more piquant, if that's the word I'm looking for. Frankly, of all the tapes, it's the one I find myself taking down off the shelf most often. It's definitely the one I'd start with, if I were you. You want to hear it?'

He surveyed his stacked cassettes blearily.

'Unless you'd prefer to be the star yourself, of course.'

'What's that supposed to mean?'

Allen slumped back into his chair.

'Well, see, once Scott was out of the picture I kind of lost interest for a while. There were others, I knew that. I can't remember the names. They came, they went. No pun intended. By that time, I didn't really care that much.'

He grinned at me.

'But you were different. You stuck in there. You did the decent thing. Just what we expect of you guys. Poor old Luce must have thought she'd died and gone to heaven. Every young maiden's dream come true. The other guys were just interested in one thing, but you fell in love with her. You even married her.'

He feigned a British salute, palm turned out.

'Good show, chaps. Although as a show it didn't seem that impressive to me, I have to say. Not compared to the Scott archive, at least. His tapes definitely get more air-time around here than yours, I'm afraid. But comparisons are invidious, and I'm sure it seemed great to you at the time. Plus technically it was a piece of cake compared with that motel gig. Cheaper, too, since I didn't have to rent a room myself. It was just a question of wiring Luce's bed-room for sound, which was easy enough to do, visiting the kids every week like I did. I bought a sound-activated recorder from Radio Shack and slipped it in the back of one of the closets. I knew she'd never look in there. Hell, I found some of my own stuff while I was doing it, a pair of shoes I'd forgotten about.'

He shot me a glance.

'So how about it, Tone? Do you want to hear you and your late wife "doing the deed"? Like I say, it all sounds distinctly underwhelming to me. Lots of talk, but where's the meat? Still, I have high standards in these things. Maybe it'll be different for you. Might bring it all back, eh?'

He frowned.

'Don't look at me in that tone of voice, Tone. Hell, we're practically related. We've both had the same woman. They've got some word for that in Spanish. We're brothers under the skin. Under Luce's skin, that is. All I'm saying is that you're perfectly welcome to access my private Library of Congress here, should you feel so inclined. For legitimate research purposes only, of course.'

My limbs felt like lead, but I forced myself to stand up. I took out the revolver clumsily, snagging the barrel on my coat pocket.

'Ah, I knew Mr Chekhov wouldn't let me down,' Allen said quietly.

He finished his whiskey and got up.

'Now before you shoot me, Tone, let me give you two fashion tips for future reference. Never wear brown shoes with a blue suit, and don't choose a lightweight Burberry if you're planning to carry a concealed weapon. Okay, go ahead, I'm ready.'

'I'm not going to shoot you.'

For the first time, a trace of anger appeared in his eyes.

'You're not? Then what the hell is the gun for? And what was all that "You-could-die-tonight" bullshit? What are you, some kind of tease? I've been counting on your shooting me. Why do you think I've been goading you like this? Jesus, I've spent all this time working on you, and now you tell me you're not going to come across?'

He brightened up suddenly.

'How about if I throw in the Polaroids?'

'The what?'

The lights waxed and then waned almost to nothing.

'I took a whole set one night she was really hot. Got her to pose in various positions. Made her think it was all a game. It wasn't that hard. Man, she didn't know *what* the hell she was doing. Next day she asked about it, sounding kind of scared, but I showed her the empty camera and said I'd just been kidding. I got about eighteen in all. They're around somewhere. You interested?'

In the dim light cast by the stove, I saw him give me a look.

'Or maybe you'd prefer the video.'

'Video?'

'Well, it was originally Super-8. They didn't have video back then. I got it transferred later.'

He searched around among the video cassettes stacked on his shelving.

'This was back when we lived in San Francisco. You know those mornings that dawn bright and clear and kind of cold, with an edge to them, and everything feels possible? You don't get any more of them once you turn thirty, even if the weather's the same. We'd been on a stoner all night long. Luce wasn't really into drugs, not like me, but I slipped some speed into the juice I brought her that morning. It was a kind of crazy night. We'd been to a party, well a couple in fact, and then a bunch of us ended up driving over to Marin.

'I don't recall too much after that except when Luce and I finally got home we were both bopping and the light was just incredible and I remembered this camera I'd borrowed from someone. I was just pissing around at first, seeing how it worked, totally into the trip, you know, focused, and suddenly she came in and started dancing to this music I'd put on. Only she had plans of her own, see, so she did a sort of slow strip to get my attention. Like I was into this boring guy thing with gadgets and she needed to win me back. Which I have to say she did, but not before I got some pretty good footage. I was a little worried about the light shining in through the window behind her, the one that always used to stick when it was damp, which it was a lot of the time with the fog rolling in, but not that morning. And the exposure turned out to be just perfect.'

He smiled.

'You going to kill me now? Or you want to see your late wife back when she was still cute? What's it to be, Tone? Don't keep me hanging on like this.'

There was a deafening bang, as if someone had struck the roof of the trailer with a huge hammer.

'What in hell's that?' gasped Allen.

Before I could react, he was at the front door. I followed him out, gun in hand. The wind had died away, leaving an unblemished stillness.

'There she is,' I cried, pointing to a triangle of white lights in the sky.

Allen followed the pattern of lights for some time.

'Must be military,' he said at last. 'Area Fifty-one's just over those hills. Groom Lake Base. Lots of secret, high-tech stuff going on there. Some kind of sonic boom, I guess. We're miles away from any regular flight path here.'

The lights receded in a wide arc, disappearing over a ridge of high land to the west. Allen shivered.

'Fuck, it's cold.'

He went back inside and I followed, still holding the gun. Allen turned on a small lamp on the shelves above the stereo.

'Runs on a battery,' he explained. 'For when the wind fails.'

We sat down again.

'So what's going to happen now?' he asked.

'I have no idea.'

'Okay, here's my proposition. That gun cost you how much?'

'Two hundred.'

'And you're planning on flying back? Well, they won't let you take the gun on the plane without some fancy locked fibreglass case that'll cost more than that. Plus I can't imagine you needing a firearm at home. So how about this? I buy it off you right now for one hundred fifty in cash.'

He finished adjusting the stove and gave me a quick glance.

'I'll go and dig out my savings account. Make yourself at home. Have a drink. Watch a video. Listen to a tape.'

He disappeared into the darkness at the back of the trailer. There were various noises, then a blinding flash.

'Smile, you're on *Candid Camera*!'

I raised the gun, and was answered by another flash.

'I like to take a few snapshots when folks visit,' Allen remarked. 'Kind of a souvenir. Doesn't happen that often.'

He put down the camera and a battered candy tin on the table. Then he opened the tin, counted out eight twenties from the bundle inside and spread them on the table like a hand of cards.

'You see, the fact of the matter is I never got over Luce kicking me out. I mean, okay, maybe I wasn't the perfect husband and father, but who the hell is? She'd married me for better or worse, and I assumed we'd stick at it one way or another and hang in there, the way most people do. But she had other ideas. You got a ten?'

I looked at him through the dim yellow light and raised the gun.

'I'm going to shoot you now.'

'No, you're not, Tone. I know it and you know it. It's like sex. Eye contact. The smell in the air. There are certain rules in life, like you can't stop pissing once you've started. And you're not going to shoot me. We both know that.'

He sighed wearily.

'Strange, that plane coming over. I'm not one of those UN black helicopter wackos you read about, although there's more than a few of them around here. But I don't recall anything quite like that happening before.'

While speaking, he reached up in one smooth movement and took the gun from my hand. He pushed the spread of twenties across the table, then lifted one and put it in his pocket.

'Okay, if you can't make change, I have a new deal for you. Let's say one-forty, and I'll throw in one of my compilation tapes as a sweetener. Give you something to listen to on the drive back.'

He pushed the cassette across the table to join the seven banknotes.

'There's some good stuff on this one. I seriously recommend side two. It's a real killer. Don't worry, this is just a copy. I've got the original around somewhere.'

He picked up the revolver.

'Taurus, eh? I've heard of them. Supposed to be good. I've been meaning to get a gun for some time. In this state it's practically mandatory to have one. Plus you never know when you might want to end it all, right? I've been tempted more than once. It's the how that always stops me. Knives and razors are out for me. I have this thing about blood. I know it makes me sound like a wuss, but there it is.'

He smiled reminiscently.

'Fact is, about the only problem Luce and I used to have in bed was that she liked to fuck right through her periods. Pills? I don't even have a doctor, let alone the feelgood variety. Carbon monoxide sounds good in theory, but in practice it always feels like too much like work. Getting a tube the right size to fit the exhaust pipe and long enough to reach in the side window, all the rest of it. It's like you want to kill yourself, that's fine, but first you have to remodel the basement. You end up thinking, the hell with it, I'll do it tomorrow.'

He gave me one of his trademark beaming smiles.

'But now I've got a gun, I can do it tonight.'

'Do what?'

There was a long silence.

'You came here to kill me, but you didn't,' Allen said at last. 'So now I'm going to have to kill you. I don't want to, you understand. I have nothing against you, Tone. On the contrary, you took Luce off my hands and gave her another interest in life. Without you, she might have spent more time wondering how I managed to make ends meet, maybe even hired a lawyer to check my assets. But thanks to you she was all wrapped up in love's young dream. Well, love's middle-aged dream, anyway.'

He waved the gun in the air.

'Anton Chekhov – one of my favourite authors incidentally – said that if there's a gun hanging on the wall in Act One, then it must go off in Act Three. We wouldn't want to disappoint Mr Chekhov, so this baby's going to have to be fired, no?'

'You'll never get away with it. The police will find out that I flew down here and rented a car. They know we were both married to Lucy. You'll be the obvious suspect.'

Darryl Bob Allen smiled.

'"Suspect", maybe. But that's all I'll be. It's your gun, after all. And I'm not going to make any stupid mistakes like trying to sell off the car to make some extra cash. No, this is going to be the perfect crime. When the gun is discovered next to your body and the rental car, out in the desert a long, long way from here, they're going to say it was a self-inflicted gunshot wound. Suicide while of unsound mind. Wife just died tragically. Guy was shocked, depressed.'

He extended his arm, the gun pointed straight at my forehead.

'It's time to move on, Tone. Change is always painful, but that's how we grow. Ten. Nine. Eight. Seven. Six. Five. Four. Three. Two. One.'

He laughed and lowered his arm.

'Mock execution, like they did with Dostoyevsky. Another of my favourite authors. The piece about him in the encyclopaedia is kind of snotty, but I guess there were some things even those guys didn't get. Anyway, the shock effect sure worked for Fyodor Mikhailovitch. Who knows, maybe you'll write a masterpiece too, make yourself a fortune. You could call it *I Loved Lucy*. "Honey, I'm home!" But listen, I want a piece of the movie action, okay?'

I started to weep uncontrollably, shaking all over.

'Speaking of movies,' Allen went on, 'there's another reel you might be even more interested in. This one was a video right from the start, not like that one I got switched from a different format. Because this one I made later, right at the end of that memorable period I was talking about before. The one when I was still sleeping with Luce for months after she'd given me the big speech she'd conned out of some book on how to dump your partner, all about how it would be better for everyone if we separated.'

He plucked a black plastic box down off the shelf, laying the gun in its place.

'I'm kind of proud of this, tell you the truth. Setting it up was bitch central. You know those surveillance cameras they have in stores and offices, real small, about the size of a pack of smokes? Well, they had them at the building where I had that janitorial job I mentioned. Now I knew that the building would be shut down over the

Thanksgiving weekend, so I stayed late the night before, disconnected one and took it home. I was still hanging on there by the skin of my teeth, see, because although I'd got the job I hadn't had a cheque yet, so I couldn't pay the deposit on an apartment. Luce offered to lend me the money, but I told her a man has his pride. And she couldn't very well insist, it being the great American family holiday and all.

'On Thursday, she and the kids were out buying the turkey. Luce didn't usually bother that much about Thanksgiving, but she wanted to make this one special, because right afterwards she was going to have to break it to Claire and Frank that their daddy wasn't going to be living with them no more. While they were out, I clamped the camera to a lamp stand and set it way back in the closet, on my side. We had a his-and-hers arrangement, know what I mean? Maybe it was the same with you. I guess it would have been. Luce was pretty conservative when it came to those kind of things. So I guess your pants were hanging where mine used to.'

He drank more whiskey, waving the tape around as though unaware he was holding it.

'Then I snagged the video player from the living room, plugged everything in on an extension cord from my workshop down in the basement, stuck a blank tape in the player and pulled my clothes along the rack to cover it up, all except one little crack I left open for the camera. So far, so good. The really tricky bit was getting Luce drunk. I knew that after a few belts I could get her to do anything. The problem was, she knew it too, and the way we were fixed she wasn't going to take the risk with me around. So I had to kind of sneak it up on her.

'In the end I went down to the video store and rented an old movie. *White Cargo*. 1942. Hedy Lamarr as Tondaleyo. One of her favourites. On the way home I stopped off at 7-Eleven and bought a big bottle of Coke and some popcorn. Then I hit the liquor store and picked up a twenty-sixer of Smirnoff Blue Label. Back home, I poured about a third of the Coke down the sink and topped up with the vodka. Both the kids were spending the night with friends, so they weren't a problem.'

It seemed that the battery-operated lamp had started to fail too. I could hardly see Allen's face.

'Well, like a charm it voiked, as they say. I salted the popcorn pretty heavily and kept topping up Luce's glass of Coke, and by the end of the movie she was pretty well sideways. I told her I'd run her a bath, and while she was in it I turned on the VCR and the camera, leaving the closet door on my side open just wide enough. Luce came back from the bathroom in her robe and nightgown. First of all she tried to get me to sleep in Frank's room, and when I started to undress she made a show of protesting, but I knew her heart wasn't in it.'

He set the tape down and laughed heartily.

'I'd bought this tape. Ninety minutes. I figured that should be enough, but you know what? It ran out before we did. You want to watch it?'

I couldn't speak.

'Well, it's your call,' Allen went on.

He sighed lazily.

'So tell me, Tone, how was it for you?'

'What do you mean?'

'How did you like fucking her worn-out old snatch?'

I finally found my voice.

'It was just great once I got past the worn-out bit.'

'Yeah, I heard that one already. Not bad, though. You've got a sense of humour, anyway. That's good. A loser needs that. Winners don't need to be witty. They've won. Humour's a loser's saving grace. And that's what you are, Tone, let's face it. A loser.'

'You're the loser, if anyone is.'

'Oh, I guess I'm a loser in the eyes of so-called society, no question about it. But in this particular little area, you are. You know why?'

I heard him splash more whiskey into his glass, then drink it.

'Because I got to fuck her when she was twenty. Not to mention when she was thirty. You should have seen her when she was thirty. Luce once told me that she would have a three-act life. Gauche adolescent, knockout mid-life and sweet old lady. Well, I guess I got the first two, while you were stuck with the sweet old lady. Plus you know what? Ben Franklin was right about the oldies being grateful and all the rest of it. What he didn't say was that there's a downside too. Same with the uglies. You ever fuck the uglies, Tone? Ever get that desperate? Sure they'll let you do it. Sure they're grateful. But they also despise you, just like the sweet old ladies do. For not getting better-looking, younger stuff. It's kind of a Groucho Marx take, you know? They don't want to get laid by anybody who'd fuck someone like them.'

There was a long silence.

'Fifteen years, Tone. One hundred eighty months. Over five thousand days and nights. When she was in her twen-ties and thirties, with a body to die for and a cunt that wouldn't quit. We used to do it four, five times a day in the early years. And everywhere. On the kitchen counter, in the shower, on the floor. One time we did it in the toi-let on an airplane. Even after the babies we still did it at least once a day. And after I left there was Scott and at least three other guys she had on the side. And then along comes you, a big-time journalist and all. And a distin-guished English gentleman, to boot. Well, Luce wasn't stupid. She could tell a meal ticket when she saw one. She never cared about money when we were together. All she cared about was me and her babies. Nothing else mattered. Nothing.'

I stood up and groped my way to the door. Outside, the night was eerily still. The wind having failed, the sign suspended from the metal mast gave no light.

'Tone? Come back. I need you, Tone! Don't leave me alone here.'

I groped my way forward, stumbled on something and fell painfully, grazing my shin. I could just make out the figure of Darryl Bob Allen framed in the faint light from the doorway of the trailer. I stood up, trying to get my bearings in the darkness, then made my way back to the car.

NOT HERE

She said, 'He said I had the best breasts at San Francisco State.' It was a casual aside in some conversation I don't otherwise recall, quite early on in our relationship, and spoken in an almost self-deprecating way, like someone mentioning that they happen to be of the blood royal, as though she were embarrassed at having raised a topic which had nothing whatsoever to do with her personally, but which she felt an obligation to disclose lest the other person learn it later from some other source and feel hurt. Such aristocratic tact can easily come to seem like disdain, however, to those subject to its power.

That phrase haunted me for years. For one thing, it sounded like a line of verse. I'd often tried to add a second to make a couplet, something ending in 'fate' or 'hate' perhaps, but I could never get it to scan.

Another and perhaps more important reason was that until that moment I had never thought of her breasts as having a past. Still less a future.

It was also notable in that, of all the women I'd known,

Lucy seemed the least aware of or interested in her own beauty. In fact she wasn't really interested in herself at all, even to a fault, I sometimes thought. She took herself lightly, and seemed both bemused and slightly amused by the amount of attention she got.

A steady drizzle dripped down on the window of my hotel room, squeezed out of the clouds I'd flown through the day before, stacked five miles high overhead. The way the room faced, our house must theoretically have been visible somewhere on that low line of hills just beyond the freeway. I'd spent just one night there after Lucy's memorial service, bunking down on the sofa in the living room. Frank had his old room in the basement, Claire the guest bedroom upstairs which had once been hers.

Even in those extreme circumstances, I hadn't managed to find out anything much about Frank, as reticent and evasive now as he had been when I'd moved in eight years earlier. His only apparent reference to his mother's death was a comment he made on the back porch, pointing at the garden.

'That's where my tree-house used to be. Sometimes I'd get stuck up there. I was like six. And Mom would climb up and haul me back down.'

His sister put her arm about him protectively. Once again, as so often in this cold town, I had felt myself effortlessly excluded.

All I knew for semi-sure – this on the basis of Frank's

age and birthday, and the family lore which held that he'd been 'right on time', unlike his more difficult sister – was that Lucy had almost certainly conceived while I was spending a fortnight in Normandy with my then-wife, trying to resurrect our doomed marriage, a stressful project finally aborted when I got food poisoning from eating the local oysters and had to spend most of one memorable night tiptoeing to the communal first-floor lavatory.

So while I was staring into the porcelain bowl, wondering if the red tint in my vomit was wine or blood, and worrying about whether I had woken Monsieur and Madame Dupont, whose boudoir was just behind a thin sheet of plywood covered in floral wallpaper enhanced with variegated stains and blotches on whose origins I soon learned to meditate whenever the emetic impulse failed, Darryl Bob must have been hurling another bodily fluid into a very different receptacle.

Lucy would have been vociferously urging him on, I knew. She'd done it often enough with me. Sexual ecstasy doesn't foster verbal inventiveness. There's a limited number of things you can say in that situation, and I had a pretty good idea exactly what Lucy had said as her husband came inside her all those years ago, quite possibly while I was puking in silent misery in a shit-stained cubicle, surrounded by strangers of whom the most total was my wife.

In this, as in so many other ways, Claire was different. I

couldn't for the life of me remember what I'd been doing at the period of her conception. My diaries of that period had gone missing, along with a lot of other things, when I moved to the States. But whatever it was, it certainly hadn't involved making love to Lucy, watching her remove her clothes and then move towards me with that look of shy, girlish greed. Of all the things that Darryl Bob Allen had told me, that was the one that had got to me most. Like him, I'd never got used to Lucy naked. I knew every inch of her body, but each time she revealed herself to me I felt as though I'd never seen her before. I never would again now, and that enigmatic absence would haunt me for ever.

It would also haunt our house, I realized, as soon as Claire and Frank left to go back to their respective lives after the service. I'd declined the company's thoughtful offer, made to all those who had been intercepted and diverted to the concrete chapel in the main terminal, of a free trip to the site, plus a weekend at Disneyland in a luxury hotel with a no-limit credit card. Now I was beginning to wonder if it might not have been the best idea. Certainly I wasn't up to spending the night at home alone, in the bed which Lucy and I had shared. In the end I moved out to the distinctly non-luxury hotel that we'd used for our early romantic trysts, before I became legitimized within the family and the nation.

An octagonal art deco tower built in the forties and since refurbished, its rooms were all identical except for the view. I knew that, because Lucy and I had occupied at least ten of them. I didn't know whether the room I had been allotted on this occasion was one of these or not, but I chose to believe it was. The view was certainly the same, but the one we'd stayed in one memorable weekend may have been on the next floor up or down. 'I think you just raped me with my consent,' she said about three in the morning of one of those nights spent making love and talking endlessly about every subject under the sun, fuelled by room service club sandwiches and a bottle of duty-free Macallan.

The décor, which had then seemed pleasantly neutral and unobtrusive, now looked dirty, stale and depressing. On the television news, a state governor defended his decision not to stay the execution of a sixty-two-year-old great-grandmother convicted of shooting her abusive husband. She'd begged him not to kill her, he said, mimicking her frail, whiny tones, so as to spare the anguish it would cause her children and grandchildren, and then went on to affirm his personal belief in Jesus Christ and a policy of zero tolerance. In other news, a first-grader had pulled a gun and killed a six-year-old classmate after a card trade deal allegedly went wrong, and investigators announced the discovery of the flight recorder from the Seattle-bound plane which had crashed into the Pacific near Los Angeles a week earlier, killing everyone on board. Details at ten.

Outside the hotel it was already dark, a dank rain falling on the sad, cracked, crow-infested streets. Down on the waterfront, I boarded the first outbound ferry. Even at night, the coastline was never out of sight, irregular lines of lights marking the shallow shale cliffs, the homes hunkered down amid the stunted conifers, perched precariously on mounds of unstable slurry. These confined waters looked like a shallow lake, but a glacier had hollowed out the inlet to over seven hundred feet, a fjord with no balancing heights. Pointlessly deep, and therefore semantically shallow.

When the ferry docked, I went ashore and walked into a bar in a grim little town infected with the same oxymoronic disease as the sound I had just crossed, a transit camp for resident aliens who had gained what they thought they wanted at the price of losing the one thing which could have made sense of it all. There was no here here, *kein Warum*. I felt right at home. Welcome to the post-meaning society. Coming soon to a community near you.

I ordered a beer from a tough-looking redhead wearing a T-shirt which read: 'Don't Mess With Big Emma'. The other customers, mostly men, were drinking and smoking and chatting and bullshitting, with the barmaid as referee and consultant. 'You want to just cross that bitch off your stress list, honey,' she advised someone as she poured my pint.

During the long drive back to Reno, I had asked myself how much of what Darryl Bob Allen had told me was true. According to Lucy, he was a serious alcoholic, preoccupied with madcap schemes that were always about to make the family rich but which eventually left her facing over a hundred thousand dollars' worth of debt. And there had been something else, something which had eventually pushed her into throwing him out.

'He lied to me. That was the last straw. It was nothing personal. He lied to everyone. He lied to himself. He didn't even know he was doing it. He'd forgotten the difference, or it meant nothing to him. As long as he believed it at the time, it was true.'

Certainly his portrait of 'Luce' as a supercharged fuckslut didn't jibe with my own memories, but that didn't necessarily make either it or them false. The Lucy he had known had been half the age at which I'd met her. What I did doubt was the existence of the tapes and photographs and videos he had taunted me with. It all sounded a little too practical and organized for a flake like Allen to have actually brought off. No doubt he'd fantasized about it, just as he had, according to Lucy, about renovating a derelict Milwaukee Road steam locomotive in their backyard, or making a fortune by leaching gold dust out of the floorboards of abandoned miners' shacks. But I didn't think it was any more likely that he would actually have brought this plan off.

No, the whole evening had been nothing but a manipulative psychodrama, a guy-on-guy grudge match designed to bleed me of every emotional drop I was good for. Which had been plenty, I had to admit. Plus I had asked for it. I'd been crazy to go in the first place, as my impulse purchase of the revolver amply demonstrated. Allen had accused me of having gone there to kill him, but that was ludicrous. As was my feeble cover story about the children and the will.

So why had I gone? All I could think of was that I must have been suffering from shock. Perhaps I still was. Having lost Lucy, he was the next best thing. That made no sense, any more than taking the ferry over to this no-hope port town and spending the evening getting sideways in some crummy bar.

The hell with it. No one was going to call me to account, and besides, I had a perfect excuse. Hadn't my wife just died? And these are not good times to die, I thought, signalling Big Emma for a refill. It's an embarrassment to all concerned, like getting fired from life. There might be an element of bad luck involved, but most likely it reflects on your performance.

Or maybe I *had* meant to kill Darryl Bob. Why would I have spent all that time doing target practice out in the desert otherwise? I'd certainly resented him. Not so much, as he claimed, because he'd known Lucy when she was younger, but because he was the father of her children. Even after they were divorced and he moved to Nevada, that fact gave him a status in the family which I could never aspire to. The subject wasn't discussed, but we all knew it. When push came to shove, I was just the hired help. Darryl Bob was a union man.

I pounded my fist on the bar, rattling the ashtrays. What had the perky, self-satisfied, bearded asshole done to deserve such luck?

The answer, of course, was obvious. Lucy wanted babies. At the peak of her fecundity, she'd scoped out Darryl Bob and decided that he possessed the necessary advantageous chromosomal qualities to ensure that their respective phenotypical genetic variations would be preserved in offspring capable of reaching full maturation and competing sufficiently successfully in the food chain both inter- and extra-specially to give them an optimal chance of procreating further generations in their turn. In other words, he'd been in the right place at the right time. All our love and tenderness and humour was so much piss in the wind. We'd 'done the deed', but they'd mated. Nothing would ever change that.

One of the men came over and plonked down next to me on the high padded bar stools. The embroidered label on his work clothes indicated that his name was Chuck.

'You okay?' he asked.

Realizing that I'd transgressed one of the unwritten laws of the bar, I flashed an ingratiating smile.

'Sorry about that.'

'You got problems?'

'Woman problems.'

Chuck nodded sympathetically.

'Worst kind. Want to talk about it?'

I shook my head.

'Only, thing is, we don't want no trouble here, see?'

I nodded, almost in tears. He was being nice to me, the big galoot. He could have decked me with one hand, but instead he was being kind.

'There won't be any trouble,' I told him. 'I'm sorry, I just lost it for a second. It won't happen again.'

He nodded some more.

'Sure you don't want to talk about it?'

'Really.'

'Okay. But if you want some temporary relief and a change of pace, you might want to have a word with Mercy.'

'Who?'

He looked around the bar.

'Oh, she's not back yet. Wait a while. I'll point her out to you.'

Chuck went back to his Bud and his buds. Instead of pounding the bar with my fist, I stabbed it with my finger.

My recent flight to Reno had not been my first. A couple of months earlier, Lucy and I had gone there together for a weekend break, and driven along the self-proclaimed 'loneliest road in America', Highway 50, across northern Nevada into Utah. The trip had been memorable for two things. One was the landscape, a succession of bleak mountain ranges and even bleaker high plateau pasturelands, punctuated at intervals of over a hundred miles by ghost mining towns. The other was the discovery that Lucy had a gambling streak.

Every gas station, convenience store and truck stop we went into had at least three or four slot machines, and every diner and saloon had more. Some had touch-sensitive screens embedded in the table or bar. Lucy had revealed herself to be a compulsive although conservative gambler. She had set herself a twenty-dollar limit, and managed to break even, but when I tried, the numbers never panned out. I'd lost every time.

Speaking of which, I was going to have to earn some money somehow, and soon. I remembered an offer from some foodie mag which I had earlier turned down, a piece on lesser-known French wines which were in danger of dying out. Maybe I should see if they were still interested. It would give me a project, at least. Remembering the song which Darryl Bob Allen had briefly danced to in his trailer, I toyed with the idea of calling it 'Vins Mourissants', but I wasn't sure if the second word even existed.

Chuck reappeared.

'Over there in the corner,' he said. 'With the big hair.'

He pointed out a woman sitting alone under an enormous television screen showing some commercial targeted at victims of Attention Deficit Disorder. Her pale blonde hair was spectacularly layered, coiled and stacked, so much so that it had to be a wig. The contrast between this false abundance and her odd little elfin face was enough to draw me over to her table. We got chatting. She agreed that her name was Mercy.

'Was Mercedes, but I kept getting these comments.'

'About expensive imports.'

'When I'm actually a cheap domestic is what you're saying?'

I demurred with a grin.

'That's Mercy as in fuck?'

Her face hardened and retracted.

'You want to use that joke, get in line.'

She knocked back her rye. I signalled Big Emma to freshen her up.

'Where are you from?' I asked, as if we were on a date.

'Who cares?'

'That's in Iowa, right?'

'Listen, you want me to suck your dick, that can be arranged. Bill Gates doesn't have enough money to make me listen to your jokes.'

'Yes,' I said. 'Yes, that's what I want.'

'Fifty.'

I handed over the bills. Thanks to Darryl Bob, I had lots of cash.

Outside in the street, the lighting was dim and poor, pale bulbs hung on occasional telephone poles. A pick-up with no lights roared out of an alley towards us as we started to cross over. I grabbed Mercy's arm protectively.

'Not here,' she said.

She led me along the street to a run-down motel. Our room, to which she already had a key, was on the second floor. Mercy removed her coat. Her body was on the same scale as her hair, which made her gamine features look still more out of place. She might have been aged anything from twenty to forty.

'Hang in there, I'll be right back,' she said, and disappeared into the bathroom. Next to it, there was a sink with a mirror over it. At the other end of the room, a large window overlooked the courtyard of the motel, its blank surface making another mirror.

I looked at the large bed, badly remade after its last outing. I had never been with a prostitute before and now I felt panicky at the prospect. It was not a question of moral qualms or fear of disease. It was that most basic of all male complaints, performance anxiety. I wasn't sure I could get it up.

I went over to the window and looked down at the parked cars and trucks below. Mercy had returned without my hearing her and was standing, her back to me, by the sink at the other end of the room. I watched her reflection in the window. The glass must have had a distorting effect, I thought, because her hair and her body looked both different and oddly familiar.

Then I heard the toilet flush. I swung round to confront the person I had seen reflected in the window. There was no one there.

Mercy came back into the room and laid her coat and handbag on the bed. From the bag she extracted a condom, which she proceeded to unwrap.

'Well, let's get going,' she said. 'I haven't got all night.'

She unzipped my fly and started searching around for my cock. I removed her hand.

'Look, I don't think this is going to work.'

She looked at me, frowning.

'What's the deal?'

I wanted to say, 'You don't smell right.' Which would have been true. Lucy had always smelt good, I realized suddenly. I couldn't analyse or define how or why, but she did. And she liked the way I smelt too. Before her, I'd had lovers, keen and bright and eager to please, whose only flaw had been an alien odour. Not bad, just other. Mercy's smell was other.

'Come on, let me suck you.'

'No, really, I don't think so.'

'Come on.'

She knelt down in front of me and started rooting around in my crotch again.

'Don't,' I said, stepping back.

She looked at me for a moment, then stood up, wincing slightly as her knees straightened.

'I'm sorry,' I said. 'I can't do it.'

She shrugged and turned away.

'Okay. Back to the bar.'

I grasped her arm again.

'No, stay here. I need you. My wife's just died. I don't want to be alone.'

Mercy looked at me with a look of anxiety which I assumed was on my behalf. Her next words dispelled this pleasing illusion.

'That's too bad, honey, but I'm a sex worker, not a grief counsellor. When the sex works, that is.'

'Listen, just wait.'

'Let go my arm.'

I did so.

'Look, you can keep the fifty.'

'Damn right I can. This is a full-service operation, but we don't offer a money-back guarantee.'

'How long does it take you to make the john come?'

'What's it to you?'

'I mean, how long does fifty buy?'

'Depends. The young ones I can bring off in less than a minute. Older guys like you take longer. Fifteen minutes is my max.'

I got out my wallet and peeled off five more twenties.

'There. That buys me another half-hour, right?'

She didn't touch the money.

'For what?' she demanded.

'Like you just said, what's it to you?'

'But you can't get it up. So what are we supposed to do, play Trivial Pursuit?'

'I want something different.'

Her look of anxiety morphed into one of seen-it-all calculation.

'Ah, I get it,' she said, sounding almost relieved. 'What do you have in mind? It's going to cost more, I'll tell you that right now. The fifty is for a blow job. Anything else on top is extra.'

'I want you to talk to me.'

Her earlier look returned. Now it was one of alarm.

'Talk?'

'Yeah.'

'About what?'

'I don't care. Just keep talking. Just don't leave me here all alone. Not now. I'm frightened, you see.'

'Frightened? Of what?'

'Of my wife.'

'But you just got through saying she was dead.'

'That's why I'm frightened. I just saw her. Well, I thought I did. Out of the corner of my eye. I mean, it must have been some weird thing that happens in the brain, you know, when the messages get mixed up. Anyway, I just want you to help me get calm. Let's sit down, and you tell me all about yourself. How about that? Where you were born, where you grew up, where you live, how you got into this business. Do you have children? How many? What are their names? Do you have any photographs? Tell me about them. Tell me about you, about your past.

Where do you live? What do you dream about? What are you frightened of, Mercy? Tell me. Tell me everything you've never told anyone.'

She seemed to hesitate for a moment, but it was a feint. A moment later she had snatched her handbag from the bed and produced a small aerosol canister which she held out towards me like a gun.

'Take one step towards me and you get a faceful of this,' she said in a voice stiff with fear and determination. 'The spray goes over ten feet and I don't miss. Just one step and you'll be down on your knees pawing at your eyes and skin and wishing you'd never been born.'

I stood staring at her in utter bewilderment. Then I realized that she thought she was dealing with every whore's worst nightmare, some sicko who will follow her around, haunting her home and lurking in the shadows.

She scooped up her coat and bag with one hand, the aerosol still aimed at me with the other.

'I'm going to get Billy. We'll be right back. If your sorry hide's still here when we do, Billy'll put you in his truck and take you out to the woods. And another thing. If you ever come here again and try and mess with me or my kids, I will personally castrate you. You understand what I'm saying?'

She backed over to the door, opened it without turning her back on me, and slipped out.

I gave her ten seconds to get clear, then left quickly and ran back to the ferry dock, where one of the vessels was loading. On board, I stayed well away from the windows, hunkering down in the food court with a hot dog and a bottle of beer. The ferry was almost empty, but I stayed put under the glare of the strip lighting until we arrived, then took a cab to my hotel.

In the lobby, a man got up from the sofa where he had been sitting and joined me in the elevator. He displayed some sort of document identifying him as a detective named Mason with the city police. I'd already fended off everyone from ambulance-chasing lawyers to television reporters looking for a human interest soundbite. It was inevitable that the police would show up sooner or later. With a weary gesture, I ushered him into my room.

Mason looked at the sofa strewn with my dirty clothes and decided to remain standing. He was in his forties, tall and gaunt, and looked tired.

'I can guess what it's about,' I told him briskly. 'As you can no doubt imagine, it's a painful topic for me, so please be as brief as possible.'

Mason measured me with his eyes. He looked like he'd had a hard day and I was the last straw.

'What do you think it's about, sir?'

'My wife, of course.'

'Your wife?'

I realized that he had no idea what I meant.

'She died recently. I thought it was that. But it's not, right?'

'No, sir.'

He used the term 'sir' in a distancing, passive-aggressive way, like a British tradesman calling you 'squire'. Another thought occurred to me.

'How did you know I was staying here?'

'I'll come to that in a moment.'

He got a notepad out of his pocket. Because of his height, the fact that we were both standing put me at a disadvantage. I cleared the clothes off the sofa and threw them in a corner.

'Please, sit down.'

He nodded and did so. I remained on my feet, striding slowly back and forth between the wall and the door. I avoided the window.

'So what's this all about?' I asked.

'A man called Darryl Bob Allen.'

'Oh, right. What about him?'

'Did you know him?'

'Of course. He was my wife's husband.'

'You say he *was.*'

'That's right. Before she married me.'

'When did you last see Mr Allen?'

'The day before yesterday.'

'On Sunday.'

'No. Today's Monday, right?'

'Today's Tuesday.'

'It is? Well, okay, I guess it was Saturday, then.'

'And where was that?'

'Down in Nevada, where he lived. But what's all this regarding?'

'Did he know you were coming to see him?'

'Of course. You don't think I'd go all that way just on the off-chance that the guy might be home, do you? He lived in a trailer in the middle of nowhere.'

'So how did you contact him?'

'I wrote a letter to his PO box address asking him to phone me.'

'But he didn't have a phone.'

'My stepchildren had told me that he used the one outside the supermarket when he went into town to pick up his mail and stock up. I gave him the number here and asked him to call.'

Mason made a few notes.

'That's how we knew where you were staying, sir,' he went on.

'Allen told you?'

'In a way. He'd written the number on a piece of paper and left it in the glove compartment pocket of his pick-up.'

'But how come you guys were searching his truck? He lived in Nevada.'

'All in good time, sir. Okay, so you went down to see Mr Allen. How did you travel?'

'I flew to Reno and rented a car at the airport.'

'And you drove straight to Mr Allen's house?'

'Yes.'

'You didn't stop anywhere or buy anything?'

'I gassed up once, and bought some bottled water and a sandwich.'

'Nothing else.'

'Not that I can remember. Is this an interrogation? If so, I want a lawyer present.'

Mason doodled an elaborate border around the margin of the notepad page.

'It's not an interrogation *as such*, sir, no.'

He looked up and suddenly yawned hugely.

'Pardon me. Well, it's like this. A sheriff's office in Nevada have asked us to make some enquiries with regard to an investigation they are undertaking. So instead of sitting at home eating some pizza and watching the ballgame with my kids, I get to hang around this place for over two hours reading the Entertainment section of Friday's *USA Today* and waiting for you to show up.'

'Investigation?'

'Correct. I understand that there are no criminal charges pending at this time, but with relation to an ongoing investigation in another state we have been requested to ask you a few questions and then communicate the results to the law enforcement authorities having jurisdiction. You are of course free to refuse, but your cooperation would be appreciated.'

I could only think of one thing. 'Investigation'. Lucy had once told me that Allen had been a small-time drug dealer at one time. He probably still was. That would explain how he financed his little hideaway in the desert and his neon sign collection. In which case, the local sheriff would have searched his trailer and seized the contents. Assuming that what Allen had told me that night was true, right now a bunch of rednecks were probably poring over nude photographs of Lucy in her twenties and watching videos of her dancing naked and being fucked silly by her first husband in our bed.

'You want to watch it?' Allen had asked me. The answer was yes, only I couldn't admit that. I'd turned down the opportunity out of pride and decency, and now those same materials were being passed around some county courthouse for everyone to gawk at, or maybe even take to the bathroom for a quick hand job.

Mason yawned again, this time covering his perfect teeth with the back of his hand.

'Investigation into what?' I demanded.

'Look, sir, I appreciate that you want to get this over with as soon as possible. Me too, for that matter. And believe me, it'll all go much quicker if you let me ask the questions and you look after the answers. Okay?'

I nodded.

'Okay. You went to see Allen. Why?'

'As I said, my wife died recently. Allen was the father of

her children and I needed to know what his plans were. I'm not sure about the technicalities of the legal position, but I was advised that he could theoretically lay claim to part of the value of the house they used to live in. Seeing as he's never paid a dime in child support, the kids and I could probably beat that. But I needed to know if he was going to try.'

'And what did he say?'

'That he had no such intention.'

Mason turned the page and carried on writing.

'That's interesting, sir, because just a few days earlier, on the thirteenth to be precise, he called a lawyer in Reno about filing to hold up probate on your wife's estate pending a claim.'

Allen had told me that he thought Lucy would be too much of a ditz to get around to making a will. Presumably he'd been counting on that.

'That son of a bitch,' I said.

'He didn't tell you about that?'

'Certainly not.'

'Were you aware that three years ago Mr Allen inherited a house in California, the property of his mother, which he was renting out for fourteen hundred dollars a month?'

'What?'

'You were not aware of this?'

'Of course we weren't. He never even told Lucy that his mother had died.'

More lengthy note-taking.

'What time did you leave?' Mason continued.

'Leave where?'

'Mr Allen's home.'

'I don't know. About midnight, I suppose.'

'The same evening?'

'Yes.'

'Where did you go?'

'Back to Reno.'

'Isn't that kind of late to be starting a long drive?'

'It was either that or spend the night at Allen's place. I certainly didn't want to do that.'

'So you drove straight to Reno?'

'No, I stopped at a motel on the highway, then went on the next day and got a flight back here in the afternoon.'

'And Mr Allen was in good health when you left?'

'Well, he was pretty drunk, but otherwise okay.'

'Did you part on good terms?'

'As good as could be expected under the circumstances.'

'What circumstances?'

'We'd had what politicians call "a frank discussion". Like I said, he was pretty drunk.'

'A discussion about what?'

'About those things I mentioned earlier. And some other personal stuff.'

The detective made some more notes. The squeaking of his felt-tip pen was getting on my nerves.

'So what happened?' I demanded.

'Well, that's what we're trying to figure out. You say you left Mr Allen alive and well at around midnight Saturday night, is that correct?'

'Yes.'

'Okay. Now it seems there's very little traffic on that road at any time, and next to none at all on Sunday. Leastways, the sheriff's people haven't been able to trace anyone who passed by that day. So we don't know what happened Sunday. But on Monday, around noon, a passing motorist called in to report the incident.'

'What incident?'

'It seems Mr Allen had a kind of mast with a vane attached which he used to make his own electricity.'

'He showed it to me.'

'Well, there were some freak winds on Sunday night. Couple of roofs got blown off on an Indian reservation not far away. They also took down this mast of Allen's. Apparently it was never properly secured, just a few ring bolts into a shallow concrete slab.'

'I saw it swaying when I was there.'

'So anyway the mast tips over and falls on the trailer where Allen lived, wrecking it and overturning a wood stove he had going. The resulting blaze destroyed almost everything inside.'

I laughed out loud, my sense of relief was so great. If those photographs and videos had ever existed outside

Darryl Bob Allen's imagination, they were gone for ever. A moment later, I felt an equally overwhelming sense of despair. Now I would never know what Lucy had looked like before she met me. Finally, I homed in on another of Mason's terms.

'"Almost"?'

'Well, just about everything. It was quite a mess in there, apparently. But a few things did survive.'

'Like what?' I snapped.

Mason smiled.

'The most unlikely, I guess, was the film.'

'Film? What film?'

'There's no call to shout, sir.'

'Sorry.'

'Yeah, it seems Allen was something of an amateur photographer. He had a nice old camera, a Leica from back in the sixties. Somehow when the mast fell it was knocked into a corner, and then a bunch of shelving fell on top of it, which protected it from the fire. It was some kind of compacted pressboard which doesn't burn easily. It just kind of smoulders, and with the lack of oxygen in there . . .'

'What about the film?'

'You're shouting again. Why are you so worried about the film?'

'I'm sorry. Allen told me that he had some footage of my late wife which he'd taken back when they were married. I just wondered if it had anything to do with that.

What happened to Allen, anyway? Was he there when this occurred?'

'Yeah, he was there.'

Mason scribbled another few lines, then reached into his pocket and brought out a brown envelope.

'As for the pictures, it wasn't anything like what you were talking about. This was an undeveloped roll, still in the camera. The sheriff's people got it printed up. There were a bunch of landscape shots, weird-looking rocks and erosion slopes. And then these.'

He passed me the envelope. Inside were two black-and-white photographs showing a man pointing a gun at the camera. I looked at Mason, who held out his hand. I passed the photographs back.

'That's how I knew you when you walked into the lobby,' he went on. 'And it seems I wasn't the only one. The weapon survived too, of course. A revolver, thirty-eight special. The model was . . .'

He consulted an earlier page in his notebook.

'A Taurus M85 Well the first thing the sheriff did was to run a trace on the serial number, which led to a local gun enthusiast and part-time dealer named Wayne Jefferson. He was shown the photographs you've just seen, and identified you as the person he had sold the gun to at a show held in a convention centre in Reno, right by the airport, on the previous Saturday afternoon.'

He looked at me calmly.

'Do you have anything to say about that?'

I envied him his calm.

'Not without a lawyer present,' I eventually replied.

Mason nodded.

'Okay, that's your right.'

'So what am I being charged with? Threatening behaviour? Possession of an unregistered firearm?'

Mason stood up.

'Like I said before, no charges have been preferred at this point. I'm simply doing a little background research on behalf of the Nye County authorities. Their budget doesn't run to sending someone up here on a wild-goose chase, so they asked us to do a credit check, so to speak.'

'So what happens now?'

'Well, I have to say that your responses to my questions have been most instructive, sir. Thank you most sincerely. We appreciate it. Tomorrow I'll pass this information along to the sheriff's office. They'll have to decide what steps to take, but I imagine they'll certainly want to speak with you. Do you have any plans to leave town in the next few days?'

'No.'

He nodded.

'Okay. Well, let us know if you change your mind. Here's my card. I guess I'll go home, see how badly the Seahawks lost this time, maybe warm up a couple of slices of pizza if there's any left. Thanks again for your help, sir.'

The mention of pizza made me realize that I'd had nothing to eat all day apart from the hot dog on the ferry. I ordered up a club sandwich from room service, but couldn't finish it. The mini-bar offered a selection of overpriced miniature bottles of whiskey. The Macallan was not one. I undressed and lay down but couldn't sleep. As at the motel that Mercy had taken me to, I had an odd feeling that there was someone else in the room. This time it even seemed that I was not alone in bed. Finally I turned the lights back on and watched crapware TV until I passed out on the sofa.

I woke around dawn, dressed hurriedly and drove to the house I still thought of as home. A spiritless rain fell steadily and the sky was as dim as during a partial solar eclipse. Jim, one of our pleasantly impersonal neighbours, had grown up in a town housing a Federal Penitentiary and his mother had trained him to be terrified of prowlers. The rectangular, tan-coloured industrial security light he had installed under his eaves was operating at full efficiency, its photocell undeceived by the notional time of day.

I parked outside the house, breathing hard. The windows peered down at me incuriously. This was what Lucy used to do, she'd told me, when she got home from work in the last months of her marriage to Darryl Bob. Her dread of entering the house was so great she would circle the block again and again, and then sit outside in the car for another fifteen minutes, getting up enough courage to walk up the steps and open the door.

The steps were dark, the porch light off. Rain dripped off the eaves into the shrubbery. The mail was stuffed into the bin. I hauled it out, pausing only over a package with a British stamp and airmail sticker, which I stuck in my coat pocket. I fumbled around with my key, a bad copy which was always reluctant to engage with the lock. Then the door swung open and the smell hit me. These old houses hoard odours like memories, packing every crack and crevice of their wooden structure. Claire had tried to tidy up a bit for the visitors who had come around after the memorial service, but the place was still a mess. It had always seemed to have a mysterious ability to disarrange any imposed order without human intervention, although neither I nor Lucy paid any attention to such matters. At the time, on the rebound from a wife for whom those were the household gods, that had seemed charming.

Now, though, I just felt despair at the familiar clutter, the lingering scent of microwaved popcorn and fried chicken, the pile of unopened mail and the winking red light of the Caller ID machine. What could anyone have to say to me that would not seem an impertinent irrelevance? The place was freezing, too. I wandered into the living area and switched on the heating I had thriftily placed on hold during my absence, something which now seemed ridiculous. Who cared about heating bills now? I couldn't remember what I'd been thinking. I must have gone crazy. Perhaps it had seemed a sort of sacrilege for our home to be kept warm and cosy now that Lucy was where she was.

I'd been wearing the same clothes for days, so the first thing to do seemed to be to take a shower and get changed as a way of trying to get settled back in. I couldn't go on living in hotels for ever. The stairs creaked beneath me in their familiar way as I walked up to the first floor. I stripped off in the spare bedroom, the one Claire had slept in before she moved out. I couldn't face ours just yet.

The bathroom seemed a relatively safe and neutral space. One of my dressing gowns was hanging on the hook behind the door, but apart from a toothbrush and a used towel there was nothing of Lucy's visible. I was about to turn on the shower when I heard another creak from outside. I opened the door and called 'Hullo?', but there was no answer. Then I remembered that I'd just put the heating on, and that these old wooden houses, rectangular arks really, always shifted and settled as they cooled down and warmed up. I went back into the bathroom, locking the door behind me, and turned on the shower.

I was giving my hair a second lathering when the spray from the nozzle on the ceiling abruptly turned into a heavy dribble of scalding water. I leapt back, so that only my toes were still exposed, then grabbed the tap and turned it off. My entire body was covered in a rash of rigid goosebumps, and not just from the cold air. I knew exactly what that sudden change in water temperature meant, having complained about it to Lucy and her children endless times before. It meant that somewhere else in the house a toilet had been flushed or the washing machine or dishwasher turned on.

I towelled myself down hurriedly and stood there listening. There was a distinct whisper of activity in the plumbing. I wasn't imagining this. I put on my dressing gown and opened the door cautiously. I don't know what I expected. This was not a burglar, that much I knew. I padded downstairs, leaving wet footmarks on the bare boards, every sense on high alert. Now I could hear the rush of escaping water more clearly, but where was it coming from? I searched the living room, the kitchen, then the office and third bedroom in the basement. Down there, the noise from the pipes was unmistakable. No, I was definitely not imagining this. This was a consolation of sorts, but one at which my flesh crawled, expressing its ancient wisdom and terror.

A pack of Marlboro Lights lay open on the kitchen counter. Claire had presumably left it there. Like her mother, she was always vague about the whereabouts of her keys, handbag, purse, credit cards and other personal possessions. As if touched by this frailty, the world seemed to indulge her, as Chuck had me in that bar the night before. What went around came around, everything you thought you had lost turned up sooner or later.

I grabbed one of the cigarettes and went out on the back porch to smoke it greedily. It was then that I saw Allie.

'Oh my,' she said in her flat, bright tone. 'I didn't know you were back.'

She held up our hosepipe, which she was using to clean off some garden equipment stacked against the wall of the adjoining house. There was no fence between our properties. Allie thought that no fences made good neighbours.

'I hope you don't mind me borrowing this,' she went on. 'Our garden tap rusted out and flooded the basement – the water line I mean – and Jack had to seal it off. He's planning on rejigging the system come spring, but for now it's down and I just wanted to clean this stuff up before I store it away for the winter.'

I nodded vaguely. Allie was always up at five, come sun or snow. It was a relief to have a rational explanation for the variation in the water pressure, but I hadn't counted on company.

'I'm so sorry that Jack and I were away when that terrible business with Lucy happened,' she went on, turning off my exterior tap and rewinding the hose. 'We hardly ever go away, but with Tracy just turning twenty-one we kind of thought we had to drive over.'

She stood below me, looking up with a sorrowful expression. I'd always thought of Allie as a mildly boring old bat, but I suddenly realized that she must once have been beautiful. Then a frown appeared on her features, which seemed to have aged from five to fifty without a hint that anything had happened to the person inside.

'But that must have been before,' she said wonderingly. 'I read about it in the paper, and I thought it was while we were in Spokane, but that can't be. I'm getting kind of confused, I guess.'

'How do you mean?' I asked, just to sound politely interested.

'Well Jack and I got back on Wednesday, right? I thought that awful thing happened on Monday, but that can't be right, because after we got back I saw Lucy right here.'

'Right where?' I demanded, with no attempt at mitigation. If Allie was going to retail the clichés of spectator grief, she might at least trouble to get her facts right.

'On Wednesday? Or was it Thursday? No, it must have been Wednesday, because that's recycling day and I'd just got back from taking my bins to the kerb. Then I looked over at your house, and there she was, standing there with her back to the kitchen window. I waved to her and called out, but she didn't notice me, or maybe she didn't want to talk. I guess she had something else on her mind. But you know the strange thing? She looked about twenty years younger, the way she did when she and Darryl Bob bought that place.'

I said nothing, but my look must have spoken because Allie turned away.

'I know it's hard to accept, but it must be God's will,' she concluded, heading back to her own porch.

Allie was a fundamentalist Christian of some variety who frequently mentioned God in a casual, slightly resigned way, as though He were CEO of the company in which she was an underpaid, put-upon secretary.

'Let me know if there's anything I can do. I've got some tuna casserole you could have tonight if you want.'

I walked back inside the house and closed the door. On Wednesday of the previous week, Lucy had been dead for two days.

Then I remembered that the memorial service had been held that day, and that Claire had been here. That's who Allie must have seen standing at the kitchen window, not Lucy but Claire.

In the hallway, the Caller ID box was still winking. The display read 'UNAVAILABLE'. I picked up the phone and dialled our voicemail service. There were twenty-three new messages. I listened to the most recent. It was from Claire, asking me to call her. She sounded distraught. Just what I need, I thought, another wacky female. But I called anyway, and immediately regretted it.

'First Jeff walking out on me, then Mom dying, and now this. It's like we're cursed.'

'Claire?'

'I'm sorry, I guess I have grievance issues or whatever the fuck they're saying this week. It's all bullshit. And it's so dumb, because it wasn't like I was that close to him, even when he still lived with us. He was a big drunk, to be honest. Plus depressive. Mom tried to get him on meds, but he preferred to self-medicate with booze. He had violent mood swings. You never knew what to expect.'

'What's the matter, Claire?'

'One moment he'd be all lovey-dovey, the next he'd be screaming at you. Plus he was a total slob, didn't shower for days on end, wore the same clothes for weeks. His idea of dinner was eating peanut butter out of the jar with a spoon, standing up in the kitchen and washing it down with beer.'

She paused to blow her nose loudly.

'I hated him. And her. You know that? I never told you, because I didn't want to be hurtful, but now . . .'

'Claire, what . . .'

'They used to fuck, in that room right across from mine. The one you guys have now. I mean had. And she'd be screaming and he'd be yelling and it'd go on all night. And I was like thirteen, for Christ's sake, never been kissed, and I had to listen to them going at it for hours, and then Mom showing up all dewy-eyed at the breakfast table and him with that kind of "Well-I-guess-I-did-my-day's-work-last-night-so-I-can-slack-off-now" look.'

'Hello?'

'Fuck them both. I hate them. I used to wish they were dead, and now they are I'm scared. It's like I caused it. Am

I nuts too? Have I inherited this? I'm so scared, so fucking scared. Hello? Are you there?'

I could hear her weeping.

'I'm here,' I said. 'Are you?'

'Yes, unfortunately.'

'Claire, what's happened? What's all this about?'

'What do you mean what's happened? You know what's happened.'

'I do not.'

A silence.

'You mean they didn't tell you?'

By now I was starting to get irritated.

'Who didn't tell me what?' I snapped.

'The police. They said they'd spoken with you. I've been calling you at the hotel and at home and you're never there. You could at least have got in touch. He was my father, for fuck's sake. What planet are you living on?'

'Claire, listen. I was out last night. I came here early this morning. A policeman came to the hotel with some story about your father's trailer having burned down. He asked me a bunch of questions. That's all I know.'

Another, longer, silence.

'Oh my God. They didn't tell you?'

'Tell me what?'

'He's dead.'

'Who's dead?'

'My father.'

'Dead? How?'

'He was shot. The trailer burned down, but they found the gun and . . . and enough of the body. The skull survived. He'd been shot in the head at close range.'

I found nothing to say.

'I'm sorry, I'm sorry, I don't hate him, I didn't mean that. I felt sorry for him, just like Mom. He was a flawed human being, but Jesus, which of us isn't? And of course I never hated Mom. I'm so sorry I said that. I'm going slightly crazy here.'

'Of course. Look, do you want to . . .'

'I don't want anything. I'll be fine. But I have a question.'

'Yes?'

'Did you kill my dad?'

Once again, I could find nothing to say.

'Hello?'

'I'm here.'

'Did you hear what I asked?'

'Yes, of course. The answer is no.'

'But you were down there, right? The police told me when they called.'

'I went down to see him, yes.'

'Why?'

'I wanted to talk things over with him, about who gets what from Lucy's estate. I was doing it for you. For you and Frank, I mean.'

'You saw him on Saturday?'

'Yes.'

'And they found the body on Monday.'

'I was back here by then.'

'But they can't tell when he died, because of . . .'

She broke off.

'Because of the fire?'

'Yes.'

'I understand now. They didn't tell me any of this. I'm so sorry, Claire. You poor thing. I wish there was something I could do.'

She sniffed her way back into speech.

'There is.'

'What?'

'I need to know if you killed him.'

'No!'

'Only they say they have photographs he took of you threatening him with a gun. The same gun they found at the scene. And they say you bought it earlier that day, and it was the gun which fired the shot which killed him. That's what they told me.'

I listened to the renewed silence as if it were complex polyphony.

'Claire?'

'What?'

'I didn't kill your father.'

She started sobbing again.

'You didn't? You know what that means?'

She was way ahead of me. It took me another moment to work it out.

'Oh, I see.'

'He must have done it himself.'

'He talked to me about it, Claire. I'm sorry, this is not the moment to tell you this. But he did. He even talked about ways to do it. He bought the gun off me so he'd have one handy.'

'And you let him have it?'

She sounded indignant now.

'Claire, this is America. He could have bought a gun any time he wanted. He happened to buy it from me, that's all.'

'But why did you take a gun there in the first place?'

I had no answer to this.

'Tony?'

For a moment, I thought Lucy had come on the line, something which used to happen all the time in our phone-ridden household.

'Who's that?' I demanded.

But there was only white noise, followed by an insistent electronic howl.

She'd hung up on me, which was most unlike Claire and probably meant she wanted me to call her back right away and demonstrate my concern. But I couldn't. My concern at this point was all for myself.

Mason had played a clever game with me the night before, never lying but revealing almost nothing of the essential facts. Which were that I was at the very least a material witness in a potential homicide investigation into Allen's death, and most probably the prime suspect.

I could imagine the kind of law enforcement and judicial procedures that went on in Nye County, Nevada. If they got someone like me in their paws, with photographs of me pointing the presumed murder weapon at the victim, they wouldn't bother looking any further. On the basis of what I'd stupidly revealed to Detective Mason, they even had two solid motives: Allen's stash of porno material featuring me and my dead wife, and his financial finaglings which had left her a hundred thousand dollars in debt. Hell, they wouldn't even bother with a trial, never mind further investigation. They'd just warn everyone in town to turn off their lights and stoves and TVs before six that evening since there was likely to be a brief power outage due to exceptional demand down at the county jail.

I ran upstairs, opened the door of our bedroom and hunted frantically through the file where I kept my passport and other papers. Whether tactfully or to save herself unnecessary labour, Claire had not bothered with this space on her tidying mission before the memorial service. Our bed had not rearranged itself, which for some reason disconcerted me. The covers were thrown back, the sheets rumpled, the pillows bore the imprint of our sleeping heads. There was the pink flannel nightdress which Lucy used to put on like a tent, flapping her arms about to get them through the sleeves, a comic pantomime which never failed to make me laugh in pleasurable erotic expectation. There were her shoes, scattered in random disorder all over the floor, where I invariably tripped over one of them on my way to pee in the night. Her clothes in the closet, her make-up on the chest of drawers, the paperback biography of Greta Garbo which she'd been reading, her knickers on the floor, her sanitary napkins in the closet.

Files from work, unpaid bills, the silk scarf I'd bought her in London, the wooden chest she'd inherited from her mother where she kept her meagre stock of jewellery, mostly featuring pins and earrings with apple motifs, gifts from well-meaning associates at work. The framed photographs of her children, our dirty laundry in a plastic basket, stacks of toilet-paper rolls from Costco, a handwritten note in her loopy scrawl reminding her to pick up the dry-cleaning.

Not here.

WINDOW OR AISLE?

That's what they ask, isn't it? Always assuming you get a choice in the first place. 'Would you care for a window or an aisle seat today?' It's one of my favourite bits of the air line liturgy, right up there with the classic 'Adjust your own mask before attempting to assist others.'

The shuttle I took down to SFO didn't bother with such niceties. It was like a subway train. You bought an e-ticket, showed some picture ID at the gate and grabbed the first available seat. That was fine with me. On this occasion, I wasn't interested in the view or easy access to the toilets. I was watching the door to see who boarded after me.

I may have decided to leave precipitately, but I'd planned the manner of my departure with some care. No luggage, for a start, not even an overnighter. I'd added my passport and Green Card, a Sony Walkman and a few tapes to the contents of my overcoat pockets, then called a cab to take me back to the hotel where I'd been staying. I told the receptionist that I'd be checking out early the next day and settled the bill in advance with a credit card.

Then I walked through to the sushi-and-oyster bar and slipped out a side door to the street.

A short walk brought me to a far grander hotel, with a line of waiting cabs outside. No one was following me, so far as I could tell, but I hung around in the lobby for another ten minutes, inspecting everyone who entered or left, before slipping the doorman a five and taking a cab to the airport. I didn't take any chances there, either, staying out of sight in the bar, my back to the wall with a clear view of the doors, until the plane started boarding. No one looking remotely like a policeman had appeared at any point. By the time I buckled myself into my seat, I was beginning to feel reasonably confident.

The other end, I had just over two hours to catch the night flight to Paris. Everything seemed to be going smoothly, but I didn't relax my vigilance. Having bought a ticket and checked in, I left the international concourse and hid myself away in a hutch for smokers on the first floor of one of the domestic terminals. Once again I boarded the plane at the last moment, and only after a careful scrutiny of my fellow-passengers. No one seemed to take the slightest interest in me, but I didn't completely relax until the 747 hit its stride on the runway and the rumble of the wheels suddenly ceased. There below us was the city where Lucy had met Darryl Bob, but it could have been a postcard as far as I was concerned. All that mattered was that we were airborne, and that from a legal point of view I was now on European soil. I even had a window seat.

Settling back into it as the plane made its turn towards the east, it occurred to me that back in the days when I used to turn a quick buck by writing articles for in-flight magazines, I could easily have come up with a multiple-choice quiz called 'Are You A Window Person Or An Aisle Person?' The idea has just the right amount of specious plausibility to hold people's interest for about twenty minutes, but not enough to make them feel bad if the result didn't pan out the way they'd expected. The reason why the distinction still held my interest was simple. Lucy was an aisle person, I'm a window person, and that's how we met. If we'd both been one or the other, it would never have happened.

At first I was annoyed, to be honest. The flight at Heathrow had already closed, the seat next to mine luxuriously vacant. Then she appeared, flushed and breathless after a mad dash from Terminal One, where her incoming plane had arrived late. I nodded curtly, cleared my stuff away and buried my nose in the book I'd bought at the airport. Even after a single glance, I could tell that she was one of those women who have learned from experience to expect to get hit on in such situations, and I wasn't in the mood to give her the satisfaction.

For all my pretence of indifference, she imposed herself on me without making the slightest move in my direction.

I pointedly did not speak to her right through the meal service. I glanced over every once in a while, though, noting a good body, concealed rather than displayed, and a serene face belied by her shrewd, amused gaze. It was as though she had already worked out the petty variation on the usual routines which I was playing, and had decided to let me make a fool of myself in my own good time.

And in the end, of course, we got talking. Nine and a half hours is a long time to ignore someone who is sitting closer to you than anyone in your own family would normally choose to do. We exchanged data, as one does. She was a marketing manager for the Washington State Apple Commission returning from a trade show, divorced with two teenaged children. I was separated but not yet divorced, no children, a freelance journalist heading out to do research for a newspaper series tentatively entitled *If You Want To Make A Call, Hang Up: Virtual Realities On The Pacific Rim.*

I produced a bottle of twenty-year-old, cask-strength Macallan which I had bought at a speciality shop in Old Compton Street, but was now nervous about trying to smuggle past US customs in addition to the duty-free litre in the overhead bin. A few glasses of that smoky gold spirit, cut with the mineral water which Lucy had brought along, persuaded me that it probably wasn't a good idea either to try and import the two-hundred-gram tin of Iranian caviar I had picked up at the airport. I went up to the galley and scored a couple of teaspoons, and we proceeded to pig in.

At a certain point in the oral orgy which then ensued, we moved on to rubbishing our cabin-mates. I soon discovered that Lucy had a devastatingly acute eye for the minutest details of accent, gesture, dress, grooming and general accoutrement, combined with an ability to synthesize her findings into a scurrilously witty and unsparing caricature.

Above all, she was one of the very few women I had ever met who could make me laugh. I don't know why, but in my experience viable humour tends to be a guy thing. Men I loathe can still crack me up, but almost none of the women I have loved at one time or another have been able to provoke more than a token smile.

Lucy was different. She would go to any lengths to avoid hurting someone's feelings, but she was never deceived and she wasn't a hypocrite, just so long as the object of her whispered monologue had no chance of overhearing it. This necessitated her placing her mouth interestingly close to my ear. I could feel her breath on the lobe and in the inner convolutions.

At one point a small, pale child came past, followed by a woman in her sixties with a grimly competent look. She had elaborately permed faux-blonde hair and a tightly set square jaw. She was quite short, with a massive bosom and midriff tapering down to spindly legs, and wore stretch pants and a glittery sweatshirt emblazoned with what looked like a combination of a cat and an angel. She held the girl's shoulder with one hand, while the other grasped a dauntingly huge handbag.

'Now there's one tough gal,' said Lucy. 'Married a bum when she was still cute, then had a bunch of kids. That little waif must be one of her grandchildren, poor thing. She's raising it because the mother turned out too flighty. She used to be herself, but that's all over. Now she's the matriarch of a clan of losers somewhere in the woods or east of the mountains. She rasps orders at them in a husky, smoker's voice, then bails them out when they get in trouble. The TV is never turned off in the house, even when everyone's asleep.'

'So what was she doing in Europe?' I asked, scooping out another heap of the oily grey roe and inserting it between her lips.

'One of her no-hope sons went into the service. He's stationed at some base in Germany, put his usual crude moves on a local *fräulein* and ended up in the brig. Patsy here knows that left to his own devices he'll screw up completely, get a dishonourable discharge and end up back on her hands, so she went over to sort him out and show the MPs a hard way to go. The kid's the guy's daughter, to be produced like an onion when weeping is required. God this stuff is good. And what's really great is, you don't even have to be hungry to eat it.'

The next of the passengers to be subjected to our collusive malice was a fortyish man wearing one of those out-door leisure ensembles that cost more than a Brooks Bros suit. He shambled past and then turned to wait outside the lavatory, which was occupied. Anxious to show that I could play this game too, I gave him a quick once-over. He had a generically benevolent, beaming face accessorized with expensive glasses and a dress-down Friday haircut. A social worker? Or a teacher? No, he had too much money for that. That slightly Messianic look made me think tele-vangelist for a moment, but his clothes were straight lib-eral baby-boomer. And the one thing I was pretty sure about him didn't fit with any of this.

I saw Lucy studying me with a slightly amused smile. She knew I'd tried and failed.

'Okay,' I said. 'Tell me.'

'A corporate trainer. One of those guys who goes into Boeing or wherever and teaches them how to "enhance cre-ativity" and "grow diversity", or maybe spot nutcases who might flip out on the job and shoot someone or sexually harass their co-workers. The point being that when the case goes to court, the company can say, "Hey, we did every-thing we could! We provided training for all our people."'

'You sound pretty cynical. Don't you think that stuff sometimes works?'

'Sure it works. It works the way the KGB worked. You can scare most people into pretending to go along with almost any bullshit you want. But you haven't changed them. People come the way they come. All that crap does is turn them into liars.'

She smiled at me.

'Sorry if I sound bitter. I have to put up with it all the time at work, getting stuck in groups to talk about "Three things that make me special". I mean, how difficult is it to sell apples, for God's sake? I'm damn good at my job, and I bet I make twice what that little prick does, but he has the power to force me to crawl around the floor on all fours as part of some fucking "team-building exercise".'

'Here, have some more malt and calm down.'

'I'm sorry. There's lots of things I love about my country, but when I see someone like that I feel ashamed to be American.'

'But he's not American.'

'What? Don't be silly.'

'I'm prepared to bet he's British.'

'Did you hear his accent?'

'No, but look at the way he's discreetly checking everyone out. He can't hear what we're saying, but he's sussed that we're talking about him and he's letting me know that he knows. You guys don't even notice that other people exist, never mind care what they think about you. You live in a culture without perspectives.'

'Yank-Bashing 101. Very good, you got straight As. Hey, check out this babe. Oh, you already are.'

The previous occupant of the bathroom had emerged and was making her way along the aisle towards us. She was a woman about Lucy's own age, or perhaps slightly younger, with long dark hair, liquid brown eyes and high cheekbones which had been carefully highlighted. She wore narrow linen trousers and a beige silk shirt opened just low enough to reveal a diamond necklace and a hint of cleavage. Her expression was sullen but determined.

'Forget it,' said Lucy succinctly. 'You don't stand a chance. Second wife is what we're talking here. Big rock and wedding band, plus those tastefully sporty diamonds around her neck. So not some cheesy car dealer's trophy. He's more powerful and richer, a kind of elegant silver fox. Maybe a corporate lawyer whose first wife helped put him through law school. Note the clothes. Understated but very expensive, sort of fake casual, but a little too studied to be really sexy. She knows the deal. She doesn't have much to say, but then she doesn't have to say much. And when she does talk, it's in a squeaky teenaged accent completely at odds with the look she's trying so hard to create. Women like her always forget to get their voices fixed.'

Lucy took my arm, touching me for the first time, and turned to look me in the eye. As she leant towards me, I had a mad urge to kiss her.

'And you know what else?' she whispered. '*She doesn't like to fuck.*'

Window or aisle? On the flight to Paris I had my preferred choice, but the darkness fell rapidly and there was nothing to see. The aisle seat was occupied by a formidable Frenchwoman of an age which was becoming increasingly certain, embalmed in a mummy case of arrogantly elegant couture. I never found out her name. Let's call her Madame Dupont.

I attempted without much success to strike up a conversation. She seemed both unsurprised and not particularly interested to find that I spoke her language badly, but I rattled on anyway, just for the pleasure of feeling the chewy texture of French in my mouth. Madame Dupont listened with half an ear and a vague smile, from time to time dipping compulsively into a designer bag containing moisturizing cream, bottles of Evian, fashion magazines and other accessories. A further accessory, it later turned out, was Monsieur Dupont, a wily-looking old bird who at his wish or hers was seated four rows back, but occasionally stopped off on his perambulations up and down the aisle to mumble something which sounded like a complaint to his wife, who dismissed it with an expressive shrug.

After the meal, which Madame Dupont fastidiously passed up in favour of a selection of deli delights from David's on Geary, the attendants settled down for the night, leaving us to our own devices. The movie didn't interest me, so I rummaged around in my coat pockets for the Walkman and tapes I had brought along. I also found the package with the British stamp which I had picked out of the mail on my return to the house. The handwriting on the Jiffy bag was familiar, but I couldn't quite place it. Inside was another envelope, and a note.

Dear Tony

Here they are at long last, the photographs you requested. Have fun looking through them. Or perhaps it won't be fun.

Anne

I remembered that during our negotiations about the divorce, I had asked my previous wife to send me the photographs of my early life which had ended up in the formidably organized and catalogued series of albums that Anne used as a shrine to the family life which, despite her strenuous efforts, she had never quite managed to create.

I opened the inner packet, which turned out not to be an envelope, just a sheet of paper folded and taped around the photographs, all of which slid down between my knees, scattering on the floor. I painfully gathered up the ones I could reach, but a few seemed to have slipped back towards the seat behind me. I ignored these for now and settled down to view what I'd come up with.

They were not in any order. The formats all varied too: larger, smaller, square, rectangular. Most were in black-

and-white, the rest in assorted styles of unconvincing colour. Some had been bleached out in patches, others had faded overall. I worked my way through them, trying to put names and dates to places and faces. Even when the prints had scrawled annotations on the back, these were usually so recondite as to constitute yet another puzzle. 'Ides of March '71 – Eat, you Brute!!!' I hadn't the faintest recollection of ever having gone to a toga party, but here was the evidence which proved me wrong.

The photographs came in random bunches, rather like memories, and it took me at least half an hour to sort them into anything resembling chronological sequence. The earliest showed me with Sally, the first girl I had slept with, and only then because she'd been too kind to tell me that when she said I could spend the night, she meant on the sofa. She was kind in bed, too, which I remembered even at the time thinking wasn't quite what I wanted. It was still a good deal better than the opposite, though, which I came across in due course with . . .

Thea? Bea? Something like that. The shot of Sally and me, taken by one of the people we shared a house with, shows the two of us on a pier in the town where we were all at university. I'm in black, my eyes averted, an existential cigarette smoking moodily between my fingers. Sally looked plumper and sexier than I remembered her, and was flirting slightly with the camera, looking obliquely up at it with a faint smile. In the one snapshot of the adolescent Lucy which I had ever seen, again taken by a college friend, her expression is almost identical.

Leah, on the other hand, stares directly at the camera with a look that seems to say 'The very idea that you might be able to pin down a complex, free-flowing, multi-faceted, liberated woman like me with your simplistic male technology in itself constitutes an insult of the kind I have come to expect from someone like you.' This would have been in Islington, early seventies. Leah had been my first, although by no means my last, example of that class of women, particularly prevalent then, who disliked men but felt that they sort of needed one anyway, and gave themselves and the man involved a bunch of grief as a way of demonstrating just how despicable the whole sorry business was.

Leah certainly had no intention of compromising her unique particularity by having children, and since the surrender to gender stereotypes this involves is symbolized by the female orgasm – I'm paraphrasing her rhetoric here – her attitude to sex had been ambivalent too. Theoretically, she'd held that every 'penetrational act' was tantamount to rape, and repeatedly accused me of 'imposing' orgasms on her. In practice she was the most demanding lover I have ever had, particularly when it came to the precise details of sequence, duration, technique and post-game commentary.

But I'd been young then, and saw Leah as a challenge which at least three other men in our circle were ready to take up any time I felt I couldn't handle it, so I'd hung in there gamely. In the end she'd pretended to come around to my point of view, having finally decided that maybe she should have a child after all. I promptly ditched her. The tragedy of every relationship is that it changes the way you look at things, including the relationship itself, which it may well end by making seem irrelevant. I could forgive Leah her endless diatribes and sparring matches, anything but turning herself into a pallid version of someone I'd wished I'd never met in the first place.

Later on I learned never to mess with women who hate their mothers, and came to regard my affair with Leah as a humiliating waste of time. Now, looking at those photographs and the others in the pack, I felt only the insidious power of the past. Sally and I had met at university, where she was a year ahead of me. When she graduated, she stayed around for most of the following year, in the hope, I discovered during the bitter rows at the time of our eventual break-up, that I would marry her, settle down and have a family.

We never did have children, but what I didn't understand at the time was that we were creating a past together. It wasn't in any sense a glamorous or interesting past, but it existed, and as soon as we broke up it started to undermine the present. The second time is never the same as the first, even when it's identical. Think of double bars in music.

The past can't take on the present on its own terms. Anyone who's ever revisited a childhood home or school friend knows that. But in this apparent defeat lies its abiding victory, because absence is so much more insidiously powerful than presence. Those places and people have nothing to say to us now, but they did then. We've lost something, and our very vagueness about precisely what that something is makes the brash, shallow immediacy of the present look like fast food compared to a real meal.

I knew all this already. I'd learned it the year after Sally dumped me and hooked up with her future husband and the father of her children. I'd tortured myself with images of the happy times we'd spent together, even when in truth they hadn't been particularly happy. But I was twenty then, and as soon as I could I headed up to London and made myself an alternative life. It was Leah who'd saved me, I realized now, looking at her picture with new affection. She'd taken me in, and for all the problems that came with her, she'd exorcized the power of Sally to get at me. That had been then, this was now.

What I hadn't understood at the time was the obvious fact that every now becomes a then in its turn. Leah too had slipped into past mode, with all the power that gave her to manipulate me even more thoroughly than she had when we'd been together. To rid myself of her, I'd fallen in love with Judy from Fulham. There she was, a sulky and adorable 'bird' of a period too recent for her hair and clothes and posture to look anything other than quaintly retro. As of course did I, in my embroidered shirts, bell-bottoms and facial hair just about everywhere you can grow it without a surgical implant. Determined not to smile and to impress the camera, I came across now as callow and insecure.

Lucy and I had talked about having children early on, and agreed that we were too old. Neither of us wanted to propagate another spoiled orphan whose parents, once it reached puberty, would seem to its peers like exhausted relics from another era. 'Middle-aged parents are like recent converts,' she'd said once. 'Too much, too late.' But I'd thought a lot about the child we were not going to have, and looking at the pictures of myself when young I seemed to recognize him. I felt paternal towards him, a mixture of patronization and pity. I could have been him, I thought, had things turned out differently.

I knocked the photographs roughly together, stuffed them into the 'Motion Sickness' bag in the flap on the back of the seat in front of me, then shoved them back. I knew I'd forget to retrieve them when we arrived. A year earlier, I'd wanted to have them, so much so that I'd even risked an appeal to Anne. Now they filled me with disgust. They represented the incontrovertible evidence that I'd always sold my soul to the past. The difference was that then I could hope to find another woman to redeem me. After Lucy, I didn't believe that any more. The only person who could redeem me now was Lucy, and Lucy was dead.

I fell into a shallow sleep for an indeterminate period, occasionally surfacing for a painful moment to rearrange a limb which had gone numb. These waves came closer together, and finally I wakened altogether and looked out of the window. There was nothing to be seen but the usual congregation of stars overhead, and a lumpy layer of cloud below that needed only a few trailer homes dotted about to look exactly like the desert I had driven across to meet the late Darryl Bob.

Then the hand appeared.

It was next to my right elbow, with something clasped between two of its fingers. A woman's hand, I thought instinctively, and not in her first youth. I glanced at Madame Dupont, but she was still absorbed in the movie. Besides, this hand, I now realized, was coming from the row of seats behind me, and what it was holding was a photograph. It took me another moment to realize that it must be one of the ones I'd dropped earlier.

'Thank you,' I said.

There was no answer. I tried to turn to see who was there, but no one was visible in the gap between the seats. I inspected the photo. It showed me in my early twenties, leaning with studied nonchalance against a telephone pole covered in posters for rock concerts and anti-war demos. This time I had allowed myself a slight smile. There was a brick wall behind, no one else visible. I was in my full mutton-chops, no-beard period, but there was no other clue to where or when it had been taken, still less why and by whom.

I turned it over. On the back, in a rather stylish cursive

hand, was written a telephone number and an address. Finally I remembered. The date was 1971 and I'd been in my post-graduate year studying journalism at Johns Hopkins in Baltimore. My best friend Pete, a History major, had come out there from the West Coast, and at some point his girl-friend from San Francisco had come to visit him.

Alexis Levinger was Jewish, but liked to pass herself off as Hispanic, under the *nom de guerre* Alma Latina. She was lively and petite, and it soon became apparent that we quite fancied each other. We both loved Pete too much for anything to come of it during the visit, but I remembered now that, when she was leaving, Alexis had told me in a joky, insinuating way that I really should come out to the coast sometime. San Francisco was a great town, she'd said, and she'd be glad to show me around. About a week later, she'd sent me the photograph I was holding now, with her telephone number and address. There was no message, which made the message still more clear.

What struck me now, though, was the address itself: '567 Claymore Street, near the Free Clinic'. Darryl Bob Allen had told me that at that time Lucy was living on Haight, just round the block from the Free Clinic. I'd con-sidered taking Alexis up on her offer, but never got around to it. Money was a problem, plus loyalty to Pete, and some-how it had never happened. But if I had, I now realized suddenly, I might have met Lucy. In fact I'd have been almost bound to at least see her in the street or at a party.

We could have met, I thought. We could have got together. We could have had children.

Until I met Lucy, I'd never thought much about children except as a disastrous scenario – a plane crash, say – which was unlikely but always possible in certain situations. Lucy thought about them all the time. Not just her own kids, but other people's. I'd seen her eyeing babies in supermarkets in a way which could have got her arrested if there had been anything remotely sinister or suspicious about her.

There was no such risk. She'd had an unforced naturalness in this respect, as in every other. However she lay, sprawled out on a bed stripped by our love-making, she looked relaxed and beautiful, like sand formed by waves. I had never met a woman with whom I instinctively wanted to have a child, and when I did, it was too late. Now I was doubly haunted, by a past and a future, both unreal: the people we'd been then, and the children we'd never had.

'I hate the past,' Lucy had often said to me dismissively. I hated it too, but with the kind of hatred which, unlike hers, is itself a form of engagement.

I must have dozed off again. A voice awoke me, a voice I knew well. Lucy was asking me to hold her, muttering something about a bad dream. That was normal enough. She had used to sleep badly, often waking at odd hours with fears I could neither comprehend nor effectively dispel, as though they'd blown in from some previous existence where I had not been a player. The saving grace in these uncertainties was that I could feel her physical presence to my right. Couples always have their own place in the bed. I was window, she was aisle. I reached out sleepily and grasped her arm, then her breast.

My hand was abruptly pushed away. I opened my eyes and realized that I'd been groping my neighbour. I apologized profusely, first in English and then in French, and was given to understand that the matter was closed and that as long as it did not repeat itself no further action would be taken. Madame Dupont even managed to intimate that such approaches were a regular occurrence for her, the tax she had to pay on her devastating beauty, and that as long as they were not carried too far she was prepared to tolerate – in certain circumstances perhaps even welcome – them, but with her husband seated just a few rows back, *hélas* . . .

I apologized again, and reflected on the fact that if I'd made a similar mistake with a certain type of American woman I could now have been facing a million-dollar lawsuit. I dared not go to sleep again. I dug out my Walkman and a tape, which I inserted. Shortly afterwards, an overhead sign lit up with a loud ping and the captain's voice came on the PA system, informing us that he was expecting turbulence up ahead. Even before he had finished speaking, the first ripples of bad air kicked in, making the plane shudder and murmur.

Someone was making her way down the aisle towards

me. The cabin lights had been dimmed to improve visibility on the movie screens, and at first I thought it was one of the suited attendants. Then I realized it was a passenger, a woman who had presumably been caught in the bathroom when the seat-belt sign went on. Despite the motion of the plane, she made her way quite serenely along, head lowered to check her progress. It was only after she had passed that I realized that Lucy was getting younger.

I unbuckled my seat belt and clambered clumsily over Madame Dupont's legs. One of the attendants ran down the aisle and pushed me back.

'I must ask you to remain seated until the fasten-seat-belt sign is turned off, sir, for your safety and that of the other passengers.'

I looked at the seat behind me, from which the photograph taken by Alexis Levinger had appeared. It was vacant. The window seat was taken by one of those big, placid, corn-fed Midwest guys, wearing a check shirt and a bolo tie. His in-flight baggage was strewn all over the adjoining seat.

It was another ten minutes or so before the seat-belt sign pinged off again. There was no one in the seats behind who looked remotely like Lucy. At the very aft were another set of bathrooms, both of them occupied. It occurred to me that the person I had seen might have been going to rather than from the toilets, so I waited until the occupants vacated them. I smiled embarrassedly at an elderly Asian gentleman and a little boy who reminded me oddly of Daniel, Claire's son, with his sturdy, capable demeanour.

I knew now, with utter and total conviction, what had happened to Darryl Bob. Lucy had appeared to him during the night after I left and he had shot himself. 'Honey, I'm home!' She had once half-jokingly termed our relationship a *folie à deux*. What happens in such a case when one of the two participants is dead? But no one except me would ever believe it. The Nye County police would come get me and strap me down in their big yellow chair. The past had won.

By now the first movie of the night had ended and there was a line of people waiting to enter the cubicles. I waved them ahead and went to stand by the emergency exit, with its window giving a view of the cloud cover below and the stars overhead, a chart of infinite yesterdays. Everything there is as it was millions of years ago, like a city in which the further you look from the centre, the further back in time you go. Is it any wonder we are obsessed with the past, when it sits on our heads like a Homburg?

On the flight to Reno, I'd been seated next to a pilot who worked for a firm which leased private jets. We'd got chatting, and I'd asked him about the accident which was then in the news where a flight from Los Angeles had gone down in the Pacific after the crew reported problems with the tail stabilizers. He was an agreeable Southerner, and I had felt able to pose questions I might have hesitated to bring up in another context. What would actually have happened? What would it have been like for the people aboard?

'Did you know someone who was on the flight?' he asked.

I shook my head.

'Just ghoulish curiosity.'

He nodded.

'Only I thought I should ask, see, because some of this stuff you might not want to hear about if you'd known any of the victims.'

'No problem. Go ahead.'

'Well, it looks like they were at about thirty thousand feet when the thing started. "We're inverted," the crew told ATC at one point. Okay, inverted means flying upside down. At which point the floor becomes the ceiling and vice versa. So anyone who's got their seat belt on would be hanging from it, strapped across their gut about ten feet off the ceiling which is now the floor. The pressure on their abdomens, plus of course sheer terror, would almost certainly cause a significant number of them to void their bladders and possibly bowels at around that moment in time.'

He was talking guy talk, reclaiming the uncontrollable with irony and toughness. He glanced at me, wanting to know if I wanted to know more. I did.

'Okay, so that's the ones who were strapped in correctly. But lots of people won't have been, and they'd have fallen, incurring various injuries in the process. The cabin attendants, for a start-off, who are supposed to be the authority figures in a scenario like this. That will spread more panic. Plus a lot of babies and children, and some old people who didn't understand the announcement or react fast enough. Also, some of the mothers probably deliberately released their belts to try and help their children as they fell.

'So you've got all these people, many of them seriously injured, sloshing around in the various bodily fluids on the ceiling which is now the floor, and guess what happens next? The flight crew regain control and the aircraft rights itself. They dive from thirty thou down to around fifteen, then pull out of the dive and level off. The problem here is that the ceiling of the plane at some point must have become the ceiling once again, so all the people lying sprawled on it would be slammed down under several Gs to what is now once again the floor.

'It's good news and bad news time. The good news is that things are the right way up. The bad news is that a large number of the pax will be suffering from massive physical trauma in one form or another. This must have been a scene pretty much from hell, and the fact that the plane once again looked like a plane may well have kind of made it worse. I mean, here's a normal boring "This-they-call-a-snack?" flight, except the place is filled with unrecognizable figures, some of whom might well be your nearest and dearest, covered in blood and piss and shit and vomit, and now screaming in agony and terror as the plane takes another lurch, then turns down into its final nosedive.

'All that lasted about eight minutes, according to the recording. Eight minutes is a long time. Ever tried counting out eight minutes? Ever tried counting out one minute? It's a long time. Anyway, finally the plane spins out of control, descending twenty thousand feet in a few more seconds, levels out for a moment, then corkscrews down into the ocean.

'Hopefully the impact either killed most of them, or at least stunned them long enough for them to drown unconscious, after which they end up on the bed of the Pacific Ocean with the bottom feeders closing in. They've got crabs the size of a door down there and squid the size of a truck. It wouldn't have taken them long to clean up. All that stuff you read about not being sure whether to try and raise the bodies? Yeah, right. Fact is, there wasn't nothing there for them to raise. Time those Coast Guard vessels got out to the scene, those bodies had been recycled. Course, they wouldn't want to pass on those details to the grieving families.'

'I hear you're wanted for murder in Nevada, son.'

I turned. The speaker was the man who had been sitting in the row behind me, the benign and affable Midwest crnci. 'You'd think they could have enough washrooms on a plane this size,' he went on.

'Listen, where's the woman who was sitting next to you? The one who passed me that photograph I dropped.'

'They still use the chair down there. None of this wimpy strap-them-to-a-gurney-and-give-them-a-painless-injection stuff. No sir, down in Nevada they just haul in the witnesses, turn on the juice, then rock 'n' roll while your blood boils and your eyeballs pop out.'

His bass baritone voice was in exactly the same acoustical range as the dull roar from the plane's engines. I noted his slim, white, feminine fingers.

'It's my first trip to Europe,' he went on. 'A retirement present from the kids.'

Back in my seat row, I clambered over Madame Dupont and strapped myself in more tightly than usual.

Window or aisle? I was not a window person any more, I realized. I was now a nervous flier. Not because of what had happened to Lucy. When we fly, we're not afraid of the crash we know is so much more improbable than totalling the car on the way to the airport. It's because flying reminds us that we're *between*. We don't care about the view. We want comfort, prompt service and easy access to the facilities. That's all that lasts, in the end.

I put on my Walkman and pressed the play button. The music on the tape was a surprise, a medley of cuts, some familiar, some not. I switched it off and opened up the machine. It was the cassette that Darryl Bob Allen had presented me with when I'd left him.

Oh, well. He'd had good taste in music, as he had in women. I listened to the compilation he'd prepared, ending with the early Van Morrison track he'd danced to when I arrived. The tape ran out, stalled briefly, then reversed to play the other side.

HERE COMES
THE NIGHT

Mmm. Ah. Oh, that's interesting. Yes. Oh God. Oh my fucking God. Don't stop, don't stop. Lord Jesus Christ almighty. All *right*. Hmm. Whew. You're awfully good, you know that?

Good? How?

With your hands.

Do you want some wine?

Wait, I'm still coming down.

Is there any red left?

I don't know. I don't know anything. Is that all right?

There's only white. Careful, it's really full.

Ah. I feel like I'm floating.

You are. There's at least an inch between your lovely spine and the mattress.

Really?

————

I've got a problem.

What?

I just want to fuck you all the time.

That's a problem? Why?

Two reasons. First, my turn-around time isn't what it used to be. When I was twenty, I could come five times a night.

I can still come twenty times a night.

It's all very well for you bloody women.

God, you Brits are such whiners.

Where were you when I was twenty?

At college in San Francisco.

Where you met Mr Right.

Mr Wrong.

I wish we'd met then.

You're whining again.

You never say that.

Say what?

You never say you wish we'd met back then.

Sorry, I'm not a whiner.

There's more to it than that. You don't even think it. I think about nothing else, but it doesn't even bother you.

I can't allow myself to think about it.

Why not?

Isn't it obvious?

Not to me, no.

Because if we'd hooked up back then, Claire and Frank wouldn't have been born.

We could have had children.

Yes, but they would have been different. Claire and Frank wouldn't be here. Are you really such an egoist that you expect me to wish that my children had never been born?

What about my children?

You don't have any children.

Exactly.

You look sad.

No, no. It's just . . . I saw this girl today. Well, this woman. On 65th, outside the pharmacy.

What about her?

She looked just like Claire.

It can't have been Claire. She's off camping with those friends of hers.

No, you don't understand. I knew it wasn't Claire, but it could have been. Like in an alternative future, you know? She looked quite similar, but that wasn't really it. The thing was . . . Oh, tell me to shut up. I'm being a boring anxious mother.

Go on, I want to know.

This girl, woman, whatever, she was just on the cusp. Know what I mean?

Jeune fille en fleur?

No, no. Just the opposite. She'd just about come to the end of that period. But she still looked sort of young and hopeful. Only I could tell she was fucked.

Nothing wrong with that.

I'm not joking. She was parking this real beater, a white Toyota Corolla from way back, dented all over and with the trunk lid tied down with rope to the bumper.

Tell me about the girl.

I am telling you about the girl. The car was the girl, don't you get it? It looked defeated, and so did she. She looked puffy and exhausted and totally defeated. And she was still pretty. Once she must have been really pretty. But it was slipping away, and she knew it, and there wasn't a damn thing she could do. She'd made bad choices and she would go on making them. Only difference was, there'd be fewer chips on the table next time out.

What's this got to do with Claire?

I don't know. I just worry, that's all.

I don't see you as a worrier. God, you should have met some of my exes.

Where my kids are concerned, I'm a worrier. That's natural.

So what are you worried about?

It's just, I won't be here for ever to look after them. And once I'm gone, you won't care.

Yes I will.

No. Why should you? All you want to do is fuck me.

I plead guilty as charged.

So they'll be on their own. Frank I'm not so concerned about. He may not be the world's greatest intellectual, but he'll do all right. But Claire's so volatile.

I don't see her as volatile. I think she's tough as nails, just like you.

I hope so. I just don't want anything to happen to her when I'm not here to take care of things. I couldn't stand that.

Oh, sweetie. Don't cry. It'll be all right. Everything will be all right.

What's the matter?

Nothing.

You've gone all moody. First me, now you. God, what a pair we are.

I was just thinking about Mr Wrong.

He's history, you know that.

No, about me. Mr Wrong Place, Wrong Time.

Cole Porter. So what was the second reason?

What?

You said there were two problems, one is that you're no longer young, dumb and full of come. What's the second?

Oh, nothing.

Go on.

No, I just . . . I don't know, sometimes I just get scared.

Scared of what?

I don't know. It's just so intense, you know? I mean when I look at you lying there. I know this sounds corny, but I've never felt this way about anyone before.

So what was it like before?

It felt normal. Like wanting breakfast or something.

Mmm. Boiled eggs. Slices of buttery toast. I'm sort of hungry, actually.

Or like shaving, you know?

I've never shaved my legs. Well I used to when I was seventeen. But never since.

You don't need to. You're not hairy, you're downy. There's a big difference.

But I used to shave my armpits always. Until you asked me to stop. You sort of have to here.

Is it in the Constitution?

Don't be snippy.

You guys are so uptight, I can't believe it.

We can't help it.

What did you mean, it was like shaving?

Time to service the little woman. English is the only language that makes shaving sound exciting. 'A close shave.' In every other language, it's synonymous with boredom. *C'est vraiment rasant, ça.*

Is it?

Of course not. Not now.

You mean sex used to be boring until you met me? That's the nicest compliment anyone's ever paid me.

Don't get too conceited. The actual sex was okay. Well, some of it. It's just that I didn't necessarily feel like doing it all the time.

Like Tristram Shandy's father winding his clock.

I didn't know you'd read that.

There's lots you don't know about me.

True.

Don't get moody again.

I'm not.

So let me try and get this clear. Sex used to be a duty, now it's a pleasure. If this is your biggest problem . . .

It's too much of a pleasure, that's all. When I'm with you, I lose track of everything else. It's like a drug or something.

You mean a sort of *folie à deux*?

Exactly.

I've felt the same thing. And it does worry me sometimes. I just can't seem to get enough of you. But you know what? I don't care, plus there isn't a fucking thing we can do about it.

There's one fucking thing we can do.

Look, you can leave any time you want. I've told you that. Is it all too much? Do you want to leave?

No.

Then stop whining. Ah. Jesus.

I'm sorry. If anything good ever happens to me, something in me feels a need to destroy it.

That's all right. Just keep doing that and I'll forgive you anything. Oh, do you think you could touch my nipples, too? Oh. Oh, yes. There's a kind of . . . Oh God, yes, do that some more. Now the other one. Oh. Ah. There's some kind of hot line that goes straight from there to my clitoris. If someone touches my breasts, I just have to fuck them.

Do you want some more wine?

Not really. You?

I think I've whined enough. Is there anything else I can do for you?

Actually, I sort of want you to put your tongue down there. Do you think there's any way you could do that?

Yes. Yes. Oh Christ. God in heaven. Ah. Stop, stop. No more. I can't, not now.

I'm so glad you don't have a beard. Did you ever?

I don't remember. I don't think so. Maybe I did.

I hate beards.

So how come you married one?

What do you mean?

What do you mean, what do I mean? It's in every family photograph. Unlike you. Little Claire and the Beard. Little

Frank and the Beard. The family Volvo and the Beard. The Beard and the Beard.

Oh, that.

I bet it felt kind of interesting, though.

I don't remember. I think I hated it.

Even 'down there'?

Stop it.

Sorry. Prohibited zone. Intruders will be shot on sight.

It's not that. There's just nothing to talk about, that's all. He was a weak person, but he was kind to me.

You married him because he was weak?

I felt sorry for him.

I wish someone had felt that sorry for me.

Look, I was twenty at the time, all right?

How come you felt sorry for him?

He was a dreamer. It took me another fifteen years to work out that he was also a schemer and a complete fuck-up. At the time I just saw the charm. He needed to be looked after. And he could make me laugh. I love to laugh.

How did you meet?

He came to fix the washing machine in the house where I was living.

You had a whole house?

Not just me. There were a bunch of people living there. One of them knew this guy who was good at fixing things, so she got him to come round and take a look at our Electrolux.

Instead of which he took one look at you, and . . .

It wasn't that quick. Nothing like you and me. Do you remember what happened with us?

Of course I do.

On that plane. You tried to kiss me, just before we landed.

That's right. We kissed, and then we exchanged phone numbers, and I called you the next day and suggested a date, and you said, 'Let's have dinner and then see if the sex thing works.'

It does, doesn't it?

It does for me.

But that's not what I said.

Said where?

On the plane.

What did you say?

You tried to kiss me, and I really wanted you to, but I saw the other people watching us.

Like voyeurs?

Yeah, kind of like voyeurs. Mind you, we'd had all that caviar and Scotch and talked about them like voyeurs. Anyway. Is there any water? And then I said, 'I think it's very hard for you not to touch me. It's hard for me not to touch you too.'

And I tried to kiss you.

And I said, 'Not here.'

So what about Darryl Bob?

Who? Oh, well, we dated for a while, and then he asked if he could move in with me, because the landlord was kicking everyone out of the place he was living.

And you said yes. Yes you said yes I will yes.

Actually, I said he could have my room over the summer while I was up in Canada with my parents. They were living there then.

Was he at college too?

He'd already graduated.

In what?

Philosophy. Not a big job market.

So he was just hanging out?

He was dealing drugs, basically. But that was kind of normal at the time. And he got some money from his parents.

So you went to Canada. What happened then?

He wrote me there several times, and when I got back he still didn't have anywhere to go, and, well, like I said, I felt sorry for the guy. Why are we even talking about this? It's absurd.

Say that again.

Say what again?

'Abzurd.'

Fuck you.

Well, if you insist.

Would you like me to suck you?

I wouldn't say no.

You have a gorgeous cock, do you know that?

I bet that's what you tell all the guys.

I do not. Anyway, what guys?

Right, Lucy, we believe you.

It's true. Oh, come here. Yours was the first uncut cock I ever sucked, you know that? Plus I love this vein at the back that looks like a road map.

Route Sexty-Sex. What's the matter? Don't stop now.

No more jokes.

You got a deal.

Oh please. Oh please stick it in me. Stick it in me right now.

Do me do me do me do me do me. Nail me.

God I love to fuck. Is that bad of me?

Did you always?

Yeah.

When did you start?

Late.

How late?

I was seventeen.

That's not late.

It was at the time. But I've always been a late developer. I was flat-chested until I was fifteen. Why are you laughing?

I just remembered this old joke.

Tell me.

No, it's too awful. And too corny.

I love corny jokes.

Well, this girl gets taken by her mother to see the doctor because she's been coughing a lot, right? So the doctor gets out his stethoscope and tells her to take her top off. 'Big breath,' he says. And the girl says, 'Yeth, and I'm only thickthteen.'

What did you do with the cigarettes?

Uh, I thought they were . . .

I left them right there, on the bedside table.

Oh, so it's my fault?

I don't care whose fault it is, I just want a smoke.

Here they are.

Thanks.

That story?

Yeah?

Something similar happened to me. When I lived in San Francisco, I went once to the Free Clinic. It was just around the corner from where I was living. I had some sort of chest infection, and that was all I could afford. And there was this young doctor, straight out of medical school some place on the East Coast, and he told me to take my top off so he could examine me? So I did, and he started trembling. And I felt so embarrassed for him, but also kind of awkward, you know?

So you were a late developer when it came to sex?

I guess so. At first I had to learn how to come, you know?

I bet you learned fast.

Mmm.

Who was your tutor? Or was there more than one?

Not really. It was this guy, my first real boyfriend, the only person who ever broke my heart. It's funny, he called up a couple of months ago. I hadn't heard from him in twenty years. Apparently he's in some sort of counselling because he can't commit to relationships, quote unquote. The counsellor told him that in order to dock with his personal angel he's got to contact all the women he's screwed over and work through the pain with them.

So what did you say?

Forget it. Well, I was a little nicer than that. But there's no way I'm going to start rummaging through my past in order to make him feel better about himself. Who do these people think they are? If you can lay claim to victim status these days, everyone's supposed to drop everything they're doing and come help you to resolve your issues. The hell with it. I hate the past.

How very American.

Well you guys are getting to be just as bad. All this post-Diana crap. I mean give me a fucking break. And at least with us it comes naturally. With you it's forced, and forced is always bad.

So what do you want us to do?

I want us to grow old disgracefully. And I want . . .

Yes?

Nothing.

We could grow old disgracefully at La Sauvette.

What's that?

My parents' place in France. It would be perfect for that.

Could we speak French to each other?

It would be obligatory. I would call you *madame* and you would call me *monsieur*. We would use arcane tenses and never *tutoyer* each other.

Jamais. Or the children either.

We'd only be familiar with the servants.

Particularly the younger, cuter ones.

Why did you have to turn the light on? The sky's so beautiful just now. All clear and hopeful.

Le jour se lève, madame.

Jean Gabin. Mmm. *Quand même, on s'en fout royalement.*

What?

We don't give a fuck. Or maybe we do. *Si on se foutait royalement?*

How come your bad French is so much better than my bad French?

I lived there.

You did?

Well, only for a year. Less, actually. An academic year.

Where?

In Grenoble.

How was it?

Basically I ended up getting mauled on the whole time by these French leftists who detested the American military-industrial imperialist culture but couldn't wait to get their hands on the product.

Sounds reasonable to me.

Or Tahiti.

What?

I saw this old French couple on the beach in Hawaii once. They were both all wrinkly and chocolate-brown and she had this very thin gold chain around her waist.

How old were you then?

About thirty. And they must have been in their sixties, but they were just the sexiest thing I'd ever seen. It was like something out of one of those old movies. Tondelayo, Queen of the Jungle.

Ah, that old bitch Lamarr.

She wasn't a bitch.

It was meant to be a pun. Never mind. What about me?

What about you?

Who would I be?

Oh, let's see. Some Somerset Maugham character. A gin-swigging consul who's gone completely native. Carruthers. Slightly balding, bad teeth, but he's very *clean* and his clothes are always immaculate. Except he can't keep them on for more than five minutes, what with the pert-breasted native girls disporting themselves in innocent abandon before his Tanqueray-befuddled gaze.

Hmm.

His brain's been eaten.

It has?

But he doesn't really miss it.

And will you eat my brain?

Of course.

Is that a threat or a promise? Where are you going?

To the bathroom. I shall return.

What was the other thing?

What other thing?

Apart from growing old disgracefully.

I don't remember.

Yes you do. You said, 'I want us to grow old disgracefully, and I want . . .' What was the other thing?

Oh. Hmm. Well.

Go on.

No, it's silly. I think I sort of wanted to get on top of you and have you spank me. But now I'm not sure.

Well let's find out, shall we?

Really?

Let me just put this wineglass down somewhere I won't step on it afterwards.

Good thinking, Carruthers. Forward planning, that's the ticket.

I love your phoney English accent.

And do you like my breasts? They're holding up quite well, I think. Oh yes, you do, don't you? Mmm. Mmm. Okay, now give my butt some attention. Ah.

Is that too hard?

No. Oh.

More?

Yeah. Yeah. Harder. Yeah. Okay, that's enough. Mmm, it makes all the blood rush down there. Do we want me to do it to you?

No, I got enough of that at school.

They used to spank you?

Of course.

That's barbaric.

Actually we sort of got to like it.

God, you Brits are so kinky. I had no idea until I met you.

You don't know the half of it.

Mmm. You interest me strangely.

Where are you going?

To pee. Then I'm going to come back and do more things to you.

You've got such a lovely arse.

Say that again.

Say what?

Ass.

Arse.

With an accent like that, you can do anything you like with me.

It's exactly the same as that painting.

Which painting?

I don't remember. Some Spanish name.

Goya?

Maybe. It's in the National Gallery. Ours, I mean. Anyway, there's this woman lying on . . .

'The Naked Maja'?

What is a *maja*, anyway?

Just means a woman, I think. But I never liked that one. She always looked kind of preening, come-onny to me. Sort of like some vested Microsoftie's wife. Okay, this is what you got, now let's address my shopping needs.

No, it's not her I was thinking of. I don't remember the title, but there's a mirror involved.

A mirror? How?

You only see her as a reflection, never directly. Well, you see her from the back, but not her face. And her back looks just like yours. Her 'ass'.

She's looking at herself?

Uh huh.

And you're looking at her.

Yes.

Well, that's what sex is about, don't you think? A mutual act of adoration of the female body.

So when we 'do the deed', you're worshipping your own body?

We both are. Me from the inside, you from the outside.

What about my body?

It's gorgeous.

I could stand to lose a little weight.

No, I love you the way you are. That's what's so great about being our age. You accept people for what they are. Or not. But you don't waste time trying to change them. Is there any more wine?

There's some downstairs. Hang on, I'll get it.

Could you bring up the mail too? I heard it come.

You want another male? You're insatiable.

I know, and you love it.

You got the hiccups?

Yes. I don't know why. Just came on.

Eat some sugar.

Sugar?

It works.

Didn't for me.

Maybe I should try and scare you.

Sweetie, you don't have a scary bone in your body.

It worked before.

When?

Don't you remember?

No.

That time at the Metropolitan Grill. You got the hiccups really badly, and it was kind of embarrassing. Then you went to the washroom, and when you got back, still hiccupping away, I was sitting at the table in a morose posture. And you said, 'What's the matter?' You still don't remember?

For someone who hates the past, you seem to dwell on it a lot.

It mostly bores me, that's all. I'm not afraid of it. But you are, and that's why you can't remember a damn thing. It scares you.

All I remember is you sitting with your eyes cast down on your folded hands, like you were praying. 'What now?' I thought.

And then you said, 'What's the matter?' Still hiccupping away like a parakeet. Do parakeets hiccup?

I have no idea. Go on.

And I said . . . I can't believe you don't remember this.

Well I don't.

I said, 'Darling, I'm two weeks late.' And your hiccups stopped like *that*.

Hold me.

What's the matter?

I need you to hold me.

I thought you were asleep.

I was.

What happened?

I had this dream.

What happened?

I don't know. I don't remember. All I know is that you left me and I was all alone.

I haven't left you.

I know.

I'm right here.

Yes. But I'm still scared.

Don't be.

You just want me to stop bothering you, don't you?

No. But this is silly.

Like everything else makes perfect sense?

You're getting worked up, Lucy. Calm down. I'm here. I'll look after you.

Just hold me, that's all. Hold me, so I can go back to sleep.

THANKSGIVING DAY

In summer, La Sauvette is a quiet, airy refuge from the touristic inferno on the coast below, the low house and its adjoining stone terrace shaded and scented by the set of old parasol pines, their trunks dividing the prospect over the lower foothills to the sea beyond into a triptych which changes subtly from hour to hour as the light strikes at different angles and the moisture in the air gathers or disperses.

But when winter comes, and the mistral blows for days at a time, it can seem the bleakest and most desolate spot on earth. The pines toss their canopies and the wind thrums and shudders around the house like surf, seeking out any weakness, seething in through every crevice, undermining all the structures of daily life with its intrusive presence. By day, the sky is a tender bleached blue, the sunlight brilliant, while the air has a startling astringent clarity. Night or day, it is piercingly cold.

My father had bought the property as a derelict farmhouse back in the fifties, and until very recently he and my mother had spent every summer there, tinkering with various bits of rebuilding and renovation if they were up to the job, or enduring the endless excuses and false reassurances of the local tradesmen if the work was something which needed to be contracted out. Now that the place was finally habitable in something like the way they had dreamed of when they bought it, they were too tired and frail to come out for more than a month or so in late spring or early autumn. In summer the heat was too much for them, and no one had ever thought about going there in winter.

So when I phoned them from Charles De Gaulle, they were surprised but pleased to learn that I wanted to stay there for a while. The realization of their dream had come too late for them, but they were genuinely glad that someone was going to take advantage.

'So how are things?' my father asked.

'Still a bit difficult. You know.'

'Must be, must be. Perhaps we should have come out after all. Sort of generally helped out and so on.'

When I had called with the news of Lucy's death, he had gallantly proposed booking them both on the next plane. It had taken me quite a while to talk him out of it, although we both knew that my mother wasn't physically or mentally up to the journey, and that she was so dependent on him that he couldn't come alone.

'I'm fine, Dad. I just need some time to myself, you know. Come to terms with what's happened, that kind of thing.'

'You could have come here. You'd be most welcome, you know that.'

'I did think about it. But if I'm in England, then everyone I know will feel they have to stop by to offer their condolences and all the rest of it. I might be ready for that in a week or two, but just now I'd prefer to be alone.'

'Of course, of course. You must decide what's best. I'll call Robert while you're on the way to Toulon and get him to turn on the heating and so forth. It'll be perishing there at this time of year, and you know how long it takes those old stone houses to warm up.'

After my phone call, I went to an unoccupied departure gate area and broke open the tape cassette with a knife I had stolen from the breakfast service on the plane. I unreeled the black ribbon completely, then hacked it into lengths which I crumpled up and dumped, each in a different garbage bin in the concourse. The tape was clearly a compilation edited from various of the many nights when Lucy and I had lain in bed for hours, talking and making love. It must have been made fairly shortly after my arrival, before Darryl Bob had given up hopes that Lucy might change her mind about him and had moved to Nevada. She hadn't bothered to change the locks on the house when he moved out, and although he'd given her his front-door key, it would have been easy for him to have a copy made first.

On the way across town to Orly, I read an article in *Le Point* about the crash in which Lucy had died. It appeared that a faulty bolt in the stabilizer fin was the probable cause. The reporter made much of the fact that this could not have occurred with an Airbus product, and that if European regulations had been in effect, then the whole fleet would immediately have been grounded.

Lucy put in no appearances during the rest of the journey, or indeed after my arrival at La Sauvette. This both reassured and disappointed me. I knew we had unfinished business, and although I had no idea what to do about it, I'd sort of hoped that she did. She had always been quicker and cleverer than me in many ways, not least when it came to practical solutions. That was one of the many reasons I had loved her. Now, absurdly, I felt that she had betrayed my trust.

Those days were some of the quietest I had ever spent. I talked briefly on the phone to people in London and New York about projects I was supposedly working on, in response to calls originally made to the voicemail which still had the announcement Lucy had recorded: 'You have reached two zero six, four nine four, eight eight zero one. If you have a message for Anthony or Lucy, please leave it at the tone.' She started with an intake of breath which sounded like a sigh, as though she mildly resented being bothered by the phone. I'd tried to get her to re-record it, but she had never got around to it. Now that that reluctant inspiration and the formulaic message were all that remained of her, I cherished them. I often called in the middle of the night, just to listen to her voice.

There were also other messages on the voicemail. Lieutenant Mason had called several times, asking me in increasingly peremptory tones to get in touch with him immediately. Someone whose name I couldn't identify left a number with the 775 prefix which covers all of Nevada apart from Las Vegas. He too urged me to return his call at my earliest convenience. Most disturbing of all were the clicks, indicating that someone had hung up when it became apparent that I wasn't going to answer. Someone who had something to say to me personally, not to a machine. Someone who had already left the only message he was prepared to leave, and would now proceed to take other measures.

As a result, I found myself paying a lot of attention to any sounds in the vicinity of the house. The road which runs along the ridge below La Sauvette is scarcely more than a paved lane connecting the various properties strung out along the hillside. Traffic is infrequent by day and almost unheard of at night. So whenever the sound of a motor broke through the incessant keening of the mistral, I stopped whatever I was doing and listened intently. Sooner or later, I knew, one of those vehicles would slow down and then turn into the dirt drive leading up to the house.

A man in khaki uniform would knock at the door,

salute stiffly, and then advise me in apologetic but implacable tones that I was to consider myself in a state of
détention provisoire pending a judicial decision on the
extradition request issued by the United States authorities
on a charge of aggravated first-degree homicide.

The gendarme in question would almost certainly be
Lucien, unless he had retired by now. You couldn't argue
or bargain with Lucien, still less bribe him. My father had
found that out when he had attempted to stop the local
hunters coming on to our property in the early hours of
Sunday morning and discharging their blunderbusses at
anything that moved. Lucien had listened with the most
perfect patient attention to my father's litany of complaints regarding broken sleep, trampled plants and two
dead cats, and his pleas for something to be done, saying
not one word the whole time. When my father finally ran
out of steam, he said just two:

'*Pas possible.*'

And when Lucien told you that something wasn't possible, according to my father, you didn't make the mistake
of trying to get a second opinion.

'You don't even imagine that at some unspecified time
in the future it might theoretically become possible, and
that hope can thus spring eternal in the h.b. No, you just
try to forget that you were ever stupid enough to bring the
matter up in the first place, and then leave the country for

about a year or so to give everyone else a chance to forget about it too.'

I knew that Lucien would come for me sooner or later. I almost wanted him to. The evidence against me was just too strong. In a sense, I was guilty. I had wished Darryl Bob Allen dead, even if I hadn't killed him. I certainly didn't remember killing him, but then I didn't remember anything much about the stuff I'd done at the time those photos I'd looked at on the plane were taken. And even if I hadn't killed him, it was only because I hadn't had the guts to do it, which made me more culpable and despicable rather than less.

I should have, I thought now. Why hadn't I just pulled the trigger and had the pleasure of watching his stupid, smug, gloating expression resolve itself into a mask celebrating my ultimate triumph? I was going to get the death penalty anyway. At least I could have done the job in the first place. And Darryl Bob Allen deserved to die, because he hadn't deserved Lucy. Even now, I shied away from the thought of all he'd had and all I'd missed. It was so brutally unfair. After one dismal marriage and Christ knows how many inconclusive affairs, I'd finally found my destined mate, the love of my life, the mother of my unborn children. The catch was that I'd found her too late and then she'd died on me, one more statistic in the FAA record books. Thanks a lot. Thanks so much. Thanks for nothing.

Sooner or later, Lucien would come to call on me. I had nothing to do except wait, so I waited. Sometimes it was light outside, at others it was dark. I seemed to be waking at three and six. The clocks in the house had gone mad. Maybe there'd been a power cut, a frequent event at La Sauvette. I couldn't be bothered to reset them, and my own watch was still nine hours behind. Who cared what time it was?

I got the Peugeot we kept at La Sauvette out of the garage and drove down to the sea, out to a promontory called Bec de l'Aigle, where I stood with the wind at my back threatening to pitch me down into the waters below. I wondered how deep they were, what sort of creatures lived down there and what they fed on.

On the way back I bought supplies for dinner. I'd planned a classic winter meal, a cassoulet with a green salad followed by a selection of cheeses. I got to work as soon as I got home. Cassoulet is straightforward enough to make, given the right ingredients, but the preparation takes a lot of time. According to the clocks, it was almost four in the morning when the dish finally came out of the oven, but by then I wasn't hungry any more. The thought of food made me sick. It made me cry, too.

When the knock at the door I'd been expecting finally arrived, it turned out to be Robert Allier, a neighbour who keeps an eye on La Sauvette when my parents are away, in exchange for using the barn at the rear of our property as a chicken-coop and general storage area. There were no eggs at this time of year, so Robert had brought a bottle of the cherries preserved in kirsch which his wife made each summer.

I think what he really wanted was to find out what on earth I was doing there, but as soon as he saw me he remembered that he had other urgent business. I hadn't shaved since my arrival, and now had quite a creditable beard. I was wearing my father's dressing gown, a scarf, a woolly hat and two pairs of thick socks, eating cold cassoulet out of the dish and drinking Ricard 51 cut with warm water. The clocks said it was ten in the morning.

Robert backed rapidly away, lapsing into the thick local patois he employed when he didn't want to be understood. I tried to entice him to stay, but the only language which would emerge from my mouth was German, which I had learned at school and almost never used since. As the sound of Robert's boots on the gravel drive faded, I realized that word of my condition would be all round the community in a few hours.

This ended any further inclination I had to go out. I locked the doors and hunkered down inside. My real fear now was not so much of the police as of Lucy. She hadn't finished with me yet, of that I felt sure. One of her stock phrases, when she left the room or the house, was 'I shall return.' She said it in a campy, theatrical tone with a heavy emphasis on 'shall' and a husky trill on the final syllable.

And she would return, that I knew. She'd already destroyed Darryl Bob. She could certainly destroy me. In fact she'd already done quite a good job.

The first time the phone rang, I ignored it. The second time too. No one had called me since my arrival, for I had been careful to give no hint as to my whereabouts. It was mid-afternoon. The wind had shifted to the south, bringing in a skittish rain from the sea. The sky was drab and overcast.

The phone fell silent. It could have been my parents, I supposed, but they were of the generation that regarded international calls as a luxury to be used only in times of life-threatening emergency. The only other innocuous possibility was Robert, but whatever he thought of my present state of mind, he would never call me. If he had something to say, he'd walk over and knock at the door. Speaking on the phone to a neighbour, or even the demented son of one, would have been a discourtesy.

That left only the police.

The third call was later. Outside the closed shutters, the sky was starting to darken.

'Hi, it's me,' said a familiar voice.

I paused, trying to control my hyperventilation.

'Lucy?'

'What?'

'Where are you?'

'Rome.'

'What's the matter? Is everything okay?'

By now I had recognized Claire's voice, similar to her mother's, but marginally flatter and less modulated.

'We're fine. How are things with you?'

'How did you know where I am?'

'I called your parents. They gave me the number.'

'Oh, right. So I guess you've told the police.'

'I've talked to the police, yeah.'

'What did they say?'

'It's kind of a long story.'

'Is that why you're calling? It must be the middle of the night there.'

'Where?'

'You said you were at home. It's like 3 a.m. or something there, right?'

She laughed.

'I love the way you start to do teenspeak whenever you talk to me.'

'Do I? Sorry, I didn't know.'

'That's what makes it so charming. But what I said was, we're in Rome.'

'You're in Italy?'

She laughed again.

'No. Rome, Idaho. Of course I mean Italy.'

'But . . .'

'Basically it looks like Dad was worth a lot more than he was letting on. There's a house in California we haven't figured out what to do with yet, plus a bunch of retro neon signs that are turning out to be worth a fortune. Frank got on the Internet and found this collector who wants to have them restored and arrange them into a neon sculpture park on his estate in Florida. We haven't actually seen any money yet, but I've basically got the green light to max out my Visa card. So what with everything I've been through recently, I figured I deserved a break to take some time off and decide what to do next. Everything's changed so fast. You remember I did that student trip to Europe when I was at college? Just a couple of weeks. I've always wanted to come back and see the place properly. And here I am. Here we are, I should say.'

'Who's we?'

'Daniel and me.'

'Oh, right.'

'We've been to Amsterdam and then to Paris and Vienna and now we're in Italy.'

'Fabulous.'

'Yeah. So anyway, here's the thing. It's Thanksgiving in a couple of days, right?'

'It is?'

'Thursday. So what I was wondering was, seeing as it's kind of tough travelling around with a three-year-old, and it's going to be pretty lonely . . .'

'Do you want to come here?'

'Could we?'

'Of course you can. I mean, I don't know if I can get a turkey. The French aren't big into turkeys, and the pumpkin pie's definitely out. But I'll do what I can.'

'Oh, that would be so great. Don't worry about the food. I never cared much about that. But it would be really nice to have like a family day together, you know? And you're about all the family I have left.'

'How are you travelling?'

'Trains, mostly.'

'Okay. We're on the line from Nice to Marseilles, but there are also a few through trains from Italy, I think. Come whenever you want. Just give me a call from the station when you get in, and I'll come down and pick you up.'

'Great. We'll be there on Wednesday sometime.'

'When is that?'

'When's what?'

'I mean, what day is it today? I've sort of lost track, being here all alone.'

'It's Monday.'

'Oh, right. Listen, Claire.'

'Yes.'

'What were you going to say about the police?'

'I'll tell you when I see you. I've got to go now, there's a line of people waiting to use the phone.'

I hung up before releasing the loud groan I had been

repressing like a fart. I'd tried to sound chirpy, but the truth was that the last thing I needed right now was Claire and her son descending on me for an indefinite period on the pretext that Thanksgiving was coming up. Even after all my years in America, I could never remember when Thanksgiving was, let alone the point of the whole thing. I recalled being given some long explanation by a friend of Lucy's, all about pilgrim settlers and friendly Indians and a bunch of other pseudo-mythological junk which instantly produced what journalists call a MEGO attack, an acronym neatly combining the symptoms (My Eyes Glaze Over) and the cure (I'm out of here). Even Lucy had taken a dim view of this 'traditional American holiday' and, once the children left, took her mild revenge by refusing to serve anything more than sliced turkey breast and a salad followed by pumpkin ice-cream.

I'd been happy in my solitude at La Sauvette, I realized. Well, not happy, but content. I couldn't be with Lucy, and I had no wish to see anyone else until the police came to take me into custody. The last thing I needed was to have a twenty-something with 'grievance issues' and her demanding toddler as house guests, with the excuse that I was about all the family she had left.

The fact of the matter was that my relations with Claire had never been easy. As the elder of the two children, she had assumed the lead role in making me feel an unwelcome intruder into the post–Darryl Bob ménage. Not only didn't they have their dad around any more, but Mom was hanging out with this like really weird English guy with a snotty accent and ideas that were like just way out there. Plus, as if this wasn't enough, they were *doing it*. At all hours. Loudly. I remembered Lucy telling me Claire's devastatingly accurate assessment of the situation: 'You used to keep this stuff for the road, Mom. Now you've brought the road home.'

That phase had passed by the time Claire moved out to go to college. There she'd met Jeff, a deceptively pleasant young man who never seemed quite able to focus either his physical or mental gaze, and eventually walked off with another woman, leaving an incoherent note about the pressures of premature parenthood attached to the fridge with one of the plastic letters from Daniel's magnetic alphabet set.

After that I saw Claire very infrequently. Lucy, sensing my lack of interest, mostly went to visit on her own, and when we did meet she failed to make any particular impression on me. Both Lucy's children had been late developers in every respect, and Claire's personality still seemed almost adolescently amorphous and derivative, a recognizable version of her mother's but lacking the indefinable quality which brought it to sparkling life. I felt sorry for Claire, but there was something about her which reminded me of a glass of champagne gone flat in the sun.

Perhaps it was thinking about this which triggered the insight I had the next day. I was pacing up and down the kitchen in my dressing gown and socks, smoking and drinking. I was well aware that in preparation for Claire's arrival I should be cleaning up the squalid mess I'd made of the place, but I just couldn't seem to get started. Everything was too much effort.

My father wouldn't allow a television in the house, and the radio reception was intermittent at best. The only station I could pull in that evening would not have been my first choice – just when you think popular music can't get any worse, along comes French rap – but the silence in the house had become too scary for me to endure any longer.

It was then that I glimpsed for the first time an idea so monumentally depressing that I immediately shied away from it, childishly putting my hand over my face so that I would not have to see what had been obvious all along. It was simply this: my obsession with the person Lucy had been before we met, her looks and her lovers and all the rest of it, was nothing but a diversionary tactic designed to shield me from an insight too bitter to bear. I had not loved Lucy for those things, which might still consolingly linger on in some archive of photographs, videos or tape recordings, but for something that could not be captured and had now vanished for ever.

I had never really been that interested in seeing pictures of the twenty-year-old Lucy, or finding out what she'd been like in bed, or even speculating about the children and the life we might have had together if I'd taken up

Alexis Levinger's invitation. That wasn't the Lucy I was grieving for; it was the one I'd fallen in love with, just as she was, no substitutions accepted.

In my agony, I tried to invoke the power of words to pin down exactly what this quality had been. You gain control of things by naming them, but I couldn't put a name to this. The closest I could come was 'quick'. In every aspect of her being – her intelligence, her humour, her lovemaking – Lucy had been effortlessly swift and accurate. That was what her children, for all their qualities, fatally lacked. The quick and the dead. She had been quick, now she was dead. End of story.

In the middle of the night I awoke, fully alert. Something had summoned me, but I had no idea what. I consulted my bladder without result. As far as I remembered, I'd had no memorable or disturbing dreams. Everything else seemed normal. The room was completely dark. Outside, the wind was still whittling away at the house.

Then I realized two things which made my skin crawl. The room shouldn't have been completely dark. When I'd gone to bed, I'd turned on the light outside the front door as usual, a basic security measure which my father insisted on. The bedroom was above and slightly to one side of the doorway, and normally a very faint iridescence was in evidence on the walls and ceiling, filtering up through the shutters. Now there was nothing.

But it was the second thing which really scared me. The

mistral had ceased the day before with the change in the weather. There was no wind. The sound I was hearing was similar but different, deeper and more constant, but also more intimate, more domestic. It took me another moment to realize that this was because it was coming from inside the house.

I've never thought of myself as particularly brave, but sometimes curiosity is more powerful than fear, and I was curious. I unwrapped the covers, which had twisted themselves around my legs, and stood up.

The first shock was purely physical. My feet were cold and wet. The floor seemed to be covered in a thin layer of some icy fluid. I reached for the bedside lamp and switched it on. Nothing happened. I felt my way across the room, arms extended in front of me, to the wall opposite the bed, then along that to the door. The current of liquid was stronger here. I could sense it moving past my feet. I opened the door and groped for the light switch. Nothing. The noise was clearer and louder now. It seemed to be coming from the bathroom, on the other side of the corridor midway between my room and the guest bedroom next door. It sounded like someone taking a shower.

I felt my way along the corridor and groped about until I found the handle of the bathroom door. And there I stopped, trembling, at the end of my curiosity and courage. I knew, with the implacable logic of a dream, what I would see if I opened the door. Once, years before, when we were still exploratory lovers, Lucy and I had rented a cabin on an island near the city where she lived. I'd gone out one morning to retrieve some things from our car. Amongst other things, I'd taken the camera we'd brought. Then I'd turned back to the house to see her standing naked at the window, reaching up, her whole beautiful body curved in perfect proportion, her heavy breasts responding to the fine, friendly hair of her pubis, her sweet face framed by her upstretched arms.

By the time I'd got the camera out of its case, she was gone. She'd been removing a spider's web, she told me later. That untaken picture was what I was going to see now, if I opened the bathroom door. Lucy standing naked under a shower as cold as the water she had died in, showing herself off to me one last time to drive me to despair as she had driven Darryl Bob Allen. There were no guns in this house, but there were knives.

I was still there when the lights came on again. From my bedroom, I could hear the beeping of the clock radio in my room, alerting me to the fact that its displayed time could no longer be relied on. The tiled floor was covered in a mobile film of water, but the door was now just a door. I opened it and turned on the bathroom light. Water was pouring in a steady stream through a long slit in the plastered ceiling, flowing out into the hallway and down the stairs.

After a fruitless search in all the likely places, I finally had to call and wake my father to ask him where the mains tap was located. That stopped the flow, but just about every room in the house was flooded, and it took me the rest of the night to mop up the water and get the carpets out on to the balconies to drip dry. I didn't resent this at all. On the contrary, it was exhilarating to have some simple, purposeful tasks to perform. In the morning, a phone call to Jean Pallet, the local plumber and general handyman, elicited the information that he already had three frozen pipes and a backed-up washing machine to deal with, but that seeing as it was me and I had guests arriving he would try and get there before lunch.

Rather to my surprise, he was as good as his word. He mended the length of pipe which had frozen earlier and then sprung a leak when the thaw came, and lagged it properly. Apparently the cold weather was forecast to return overnight. 'There might even be snow,' he said, in the monitory tones of someone announcing an imminent hurricane. After paying him, I asked if he knew anywhere I might be able to get a fresh turkey. He gave me one of those 'Sont fous, les Anglais' looks, but said he'd make enquiries and call me later.

In the event, it wasn't Jean who called but a small-holding farmer he had contacted who raised a few turkeys. He named an exorbitant price, which I agreed to, on condition that the bird be delivered to La Sauvette plucked, gutted and oven-ready. I didn't know when Claire's train might arrive, but I knew that she and Daniel would be tired after their journey, and I didn't want to risk leaving the house and missing her call, leaving them shivering on the platform listening to an endless ringing tone.

It had been raining all day, but when Claire finally called at around seven, the downpour had intensified into a deluge which reminded me of the scene in the house the night before. The steep hill roads had turned into torrents, the habitually arid soil looked unpleasantly greasy and liable to landslips, while in the station parking lot raindrops plashed back up off the asphalt surface like shot.

There they were, standing waiting under the eaves of the station building. Claire looked even more exhausted and defeated than I had anticipated. Daniel was whining continually and seemed confused. We all greeted each other briefly and drove off, making strained conversation. I stopped at a couple of shops in town to pick up further supplies, then headed reluctantly back to the car where mother and son were already snapping at each other. I had the horrible feeling that we all knew that this had been a big mistake, but could not of course admit it to each other.

Back at La Sauvette, things improved slightly. Daniel initially seemed appalled by the absence of a television, rather as though he had discovered that the house had no roof. In desperation, I brought out some old Swiss clockwork toys which my father had owned as a child, and which for all I knew were now worth as much as Darryl Bob's neon sign collection. But as far as I'm concerned, toys are meant to be played with. I demonstrated them to Daniel and showed him how to wind them up. He settled down on the kitchen floor, staring in fascinated horror at the tin trams and automobiles and military robots, while I shamelessly warmed up the remains of the week-old cassoulet and Claire went to unpack and freshen up.

When she reappeared, we ate and listened to Daniel's enthusiastic comments about my father's toys, which were in some telegraphic version of American English I could only understand in Claire's translation. Both she and I focused gladly on this distraction, deferring any reference to other matters which neither of us felt up to dealing with. We all went to bed early. When I locked up, I noted that the rain was turning to sleet. It looked as though Jean had been right about the weather changing.

By morning, it was apparent that he had. The sky had cleared, leaving a skein of high cirrus against the pale blue sky, while the ground was covered with a light sprinkling of snow. To make matters worse, the furnace had cut out overnight, so the house was freezing. Claire was still asleep, but Daniel was on the prowl in his pyjamas. He seemed oblivious to the cold, but I restarted the furnace and then got him interested in the business of laying and lighting the fire. Once the logs had caught and were glowing nicely, we moved on to dressing the turkey. This was an operation I'd always found vaguely erotic: the creature lying on its back, wings spread and thighs raised and tied, the orifice open for stuffing. With Daniel around it seemed less sexy but more fun, certainly more messy.

I laid some bacon rashers over the bird's back, then tucked it in the oven. Daniel kept darting back to the fire, where I had to keep an eye on him, since my father was of the opinion that fireguards were for sissies. Nevertheless we had a good time, at one point collaborating on burning up the copy of the magazine I had bought in Paris, page by page. Once that show was over, we went outside to collect the basket of vegetables I'd left overnight in the car. Daniel was at first scared and then enchanted by the snow, and I realized that it might well be the first he had ever seen.

Back inside, Claire had now appeared, wearing a white towelling robe over a pink flannel nightdress which was slightly too long for her. Daniel gave her a long and, to me, incomprehensible account of his adventures while I made some coffee and put out bread and butter and jam. I very badly wanted to ask Claire what she had to tell me about her talk with the American police, but there was a new quality to her silences, a nuanced reticence, which made me hesitate. In the end I decided to let her bring up the subject in her own good time.

'Where did you get that nightdress?' I said instead.

She blushed charmingly, a brief flashback to the Claire I remembered. Her pale freckly skin had always made her a good blusher.

'It's Mom's. I finally felt strong enough to go round to

the house and go through her stuff. I mean, I know you didn't want to, right? A lot of it I ditched, of course, and the good stuff I packed up and stored down in the basement. We can go through it all some time later on and see what we want to do.'

She fingered the lace neck of the nightdress.

'But this, I don't know, I couldn't bring myself to put it out for the Goodwill, and it would be stupid to put it in with the jewellery and stuff, so I decided to wear it. Is that all right?'

'Of course.'

It occurred to me for the first time to wonder why Lucy hadn't taken that nightdress with her on her fatal trip to the trade fair in Los Angeles. It was in a heavy pink flannel made in Austria, full-length, with buttons up to the lace collar. Cosy, comfy and resolutely unsexy, she'd always claimed that it was her favourite. But then perhaps she'd wanted to have something more alluring to wear to bed when she was out of town, I thought, disgusted at myself for even entertaining the idea.

'I managed to get a turkey,' I told Claire. 'A real one. It was still alive yesterday, so it should be good.'

'Fabulous. Can I smoke?'

'This is France. You can do what you like.'

She laughed and lit up.

'I was planning to have the meal as a latish lunch. Is that all right?'

'Whatever. I want you to make the decisions. This trip has been great, but there's been so much planning and schedules and packing and what and where and when that I'm having a hard time choosing what magazine to read, never mind anything else. And it does get exhausting having Daniel around all the time, particularly when you don't speak the language.'

After breakfast I plugged Daniel back in with the clock-work toys while his mother got dressed. She then got him wrapped up in several layers of clothing, which made him look like a miniature Michelin man. I had proposed a mid-morning walk up to a restored chapel on a peak behind the house as an appetizer, and warned Claire that it would be cold.

We started off about half past ten, along one of the old mule tracks which criss-cross the area. It soon became obvious that Daniel wasn't up to negotiating the uneven, snow covered ground, and after Claire had held out her hand to him and said, 'Up again, Daniel! Up again!' for the tenth time, I volunteered to carry him. He didn't like the idea at first, and kept asking for his daddy, but once it was made clear to him that the alternative was walking, he made the best of it.

I won his heart in an encounter with one of the half-feral dogs which haunt these paths, their provenance always unclear. This was a huge black cur which came at us, barking furiously. I set Daniel down, picked up a loose rock and hurled it at the beast. Thanks to the primitive baseball skills I had learned from playing in the backyard with Frank, I got lucky and connected first time. The hound slunk away into the undergrowth, whining piteously, and Daniel gave me a 'My hero' look, and then of course wanted the black dog to come back so that he could have a go too.

Further along, the *garrigue* started closing in, a stunted jungle topped by the scrubby holm oaks and dwarf pines which have taken over the landscape since a severe frost killed off the olive trees two decades ago. As always in this landscape, the skull of rock was visible beneath the shallow skin of vegetation.

'The police came to see me,' Claire said.

I hugged Daniel and kept walking.

'An officer from that county in Nevada where Dad died.'

'They finally got it together to send someone up?'

She didn't reply. The track had become steep, and we had to watch our footing on the snowy ground.

'They seemed to think that you might have done it,' Claire said at last.

I glanced at her, but she wasn't looking at me.

'I didn't. I told you that on the phone. And it's true.'

'They said they had a ton of evidence. Those photographs of you holding the gun which killed him. And then of course you leaving the country didn't look too good.'

'Kildim,' echoed Daniel.

'I didn't do it, Claire. They'll never believe me, but I want you to. It's important to me.'

She stopped now and looked at me.

'I do believe you.'

I felt tears in my eyes.

'Thank you,' I said.

'And so do they.'

'The police? Of course they don't. They think I'm guilty as hell.'

'Not any more.'

'What do you mean?'

'When they talked to me, I told them that you couldn't have done it.'

I laughed sarcastically.

'Well that's very sweet of you. Great to have a character witness on my side, but if they ever get their hands on me they'll go ahead and fry me just the same.'

'You don't understand.'

'Understand what?'

'I told them it was impossible for you to have killed him, because he called me from a bar somewhere on Monday, the day after you got back to town and checked into that hotel. So he was alive then, which means you couldn't have done it.'

We looked at each other in silence for a long moment. The air was very still and the whole landscape seemed to be listening intently.

'He called you?'

'That's what I told the police.'

'Yes, but did he really?'

She looked at me in a way I had seen her do at Daniel, a mixture of affection and exasperation.

'That's what I told them. And they believed me. The guy even sounded relieved. I think that plane ticket to Seattle just about bust their budget. When I told him that Dad had been a depressive drunk, he said, "I'm sorry to hear that, ma'am. We won't bother you again." So you're off the hook. No longer a suspect. There aren't any suspects. They're calling it a self-inflicted gunshot wound.'

I ought to have felt an immense sense of relief, but I didn't. On the contrary, I realized that I'd been counting on the police coming to arrest me, just as I'd been counting on Lucy coming to haunt me. Now they'd both let me down. I was going to have to struggle along as I had for the past days, a downward spiral of booze, indolence and despair with no end in sight.

When the track emerged from the scrub, the wind made itself felt for the first time. Flurries of snow were whirling about as we climbed the steps to the balcony of the little chapel whose name I could never remember, Notre Dame de something or other. I set down Daniel and started making a snowman with him while Claire leant on the railing and admired the view.

'Who's that?' she said.

I bunged another fistful of the dry, powdery snow on to our figurine, rubbing it to make it cohere.

'Who?'

'That woman.'

I stood and looked.

'I don't see anyone.'

'Standing there on the path staring at us.'

I followed Claire's pointed hand. There was no one there.

'Oh, just one of the locals,' I said casually. 'This is a short cut to the village. The road's probably icy. It almost never snows here, and when it does the whole place grinds to a halt.'

I realized I was babbling, and turned back to help Daniel finish our project with two sticks for arms and pieces of gravel for eyes.

Our Thanksgiving meal turned out to be a great success. We started off with some sea urchins I'd bought the day before. Claire was at first suspicious of the bright orange, fruit-like innards, but was soon won round. Daniel spat his only spoonful out, but was fascinated by the spiny black mines as toys, particularly after one pricked him and made him bleed and he discovered that he was allowed to take his revenge by stomping on each half-shell as soon as Claire or I emptied it, smashing it to pieces on the kitchen floor.

After this, the turkey with mash and gravy came as a familiar relief, and by the time we'd worked our way through the cheeses and Madame Allier's cherries with a dollop of *crème fraîche*, not to mention a couple of bottles from my father's cellar, everyone was feeling pleasantly drowsy. Claire tucked Daniel into the camp bed I'd set up for him in her room and then returned to the kitchen, where I'd thrown another log on the fire.

'Listen, I was wondering,' she said.

'Yes?'

'Well, I've sort of got a favour to ask. I don't want you to think this is why I came or anything. I hadn't even thought of it before, to be honest. Only seeing you get along so well with Daniel, it just sort of occurred to me.'

'Go on.'

'Well, you remember last night I was talking about how we'd been in Paris? What I didn't tell you was that I met someone there.'

I looked at her in genuine surprise.

'You did? Good for you.'

'His name's Jean-Claude. He works in marketing French cheese overseas, kind of like Mom did with Washington apples. He speaks pretty good English with this incredibly cute kind of Jacques Cousteau accent. He's been to the States a million times and loves America.'

'And Americans.'

She blushed once again.

'How old?' I asked.

'A couple of years older than me.'

'Married?'

'Oh, stop being the surrogate father! The answer is no.'

'Where did you meet?'

'At a club.'

'With Daniel?'

'Of course not. The hotel we were staying at had a baby-sitting service, so I took advantage. This really nice black woman. She talked to Daniel in French and he talked back in his version of English. They got along like a house on fire and I went out and strutted my stuff.'

I poured us both more wine. Claire lit a cigarette and offered me one, which I accepted.

'I've been feeling pretty wretched and rejected since Jeff dumped me. In fact, to be honest, I'd just about come to terms with the fact that I might never get laid again. Until Jean-Claude.'

'It can't be easy to start an affair with a three-year-old in tow.'

'Tell me about it.'

'Does Jean-Claude know about Daniel?'

She beamed.

'Yes! And he thinks he's adorable. We even all went out together to a park once. But it was kind of tough his not being able to spend the night. We just want to be alone, you know what I mean?'

I nodded.

'Like you and Mom when you first got together,' Claire added, ever so slightly pointedly.

'So now you'd like to go back to Paris, leaving Daniel here with me, right?'

'It'd only be for the weekend. He's all potty-trained, so it's fairly low maintenance. It's just a question of having someone to keep an eye on him, really. But if you don't feel up to it, I'll completely understand.'

'Won't he miss you?'

'Oh, he'll fuss for ten minutes after I leave, then forget all about me. Besides, if I don't do this, or something like it, I think I might go nuts. How's he going to like having a nutty mother?'

'Good point. All right, when do you want to go?'

'You'll do it?'

'There's a train to Marseilles every hour. From there you pick up the TGV and you'll be in Paris in no time. Do you want to go tonight?'

'No, no. Tomorrow will be great. Wow, thank you so much!'

Once Daniel woke up from his nap, I spent the late afternoon teaching him the rudiments of soccer in the garage downstairs, using a beach ball and two old paint tins for a goal. Once I got him to realize that the object of the game was not to crush the ball like a sea urchin, he caught on quite quickly. That wore him out again, and after an early supper of cold turkey and some of my dad's dwindling hoard of Heinz baked beans, he went happily off to bed. Once he was soundly asleep, Claire read for a bit, but soon started yawning. She wanted to make an early start in the morning, so she excused herself and went off to the room she was sharing with her son, leaving me alone.

I seemed to be the only person who couldn't sleep. I found myself rather missing the mistral. By contrast with that external turbulence, the house had been gifted with an illusory inner calm which had now turned into mere stagnation. To add the stupor of sleep seemed intolerable, a surrender to mindless inertia only a breath away from death. So I stayed up, battling sleep by pacing, drinking, smoking Claire's cigarettes, and reminding myself that she had been prescribed glasses for her distance vision when she was fifteen, but had been too vain or feckless ever to wear them. Inevitably, sleep won.

I got undressed and went to the bathroom, not switching on the light in the hallway. Daniel had developed night terrors since his father left, Claire had told me. Our agreed solution was to leave the door to the guest bedroom open, with a small table lamp plugged into one of the sockets in the hall and turned on all night. This created enough light in their room to avoid him having a panic attack if he woke, but not enough to keep his mother awake.

I padded along the tiled floor to the bathroom, closed the door quietly, turned on the light and peed. In the black plastic garbage bin beside the sink, on top of a mound of used tissues and other junk, was a long empty paper cylinder, torn at one end, with 'Tampax' printed on it in green lettering. I smiled wryly at the thought that Jean-Claude's romantic weekend might prove to be more problematic than he had anticipated.

I flushed the toilet and waited until the cistern had refilled and all noise ceased. Then I turned off the light, stepped out into the passage and started back to my room.

'Sweetie?'

The voice came from the open door into the room where Claire and Daniel lay asleep. I recognized it immediately. I walked over to the open door and looked inside, but my eyes hadn't yet adjusted from the bright light in the bathroom, and I could make nothing out. I was about to leave when the voice resumed, low and drowsy.

'What are you doing? Come to bed. It's my period, so we can't fool around, but I need you to hold me. I had this dream that you left me and I was all alone. Just come and hold me, so I can get back to sleep.'

I stepped cautiously into the room, one pace at a time. By now I could make out Daniel lying sprawled on the camp bed, the covers thrown off. I picked them up and replaced them. Then I turned to the other bed, where a hunched figure lay on the far side, Lucy's side. I crossed over and then lay down as gently as I could on top of the covers. After a moment, a warm head came to rest on my left shoulder, tickling me with its mass of frizzy hair, and sighed contentedly.

After a while, my feet started to get cold. My father had programmed the furnace to turn itself off at night, and I had not bothered to reset it. I rolled over and started to get up. The figure to my right stirred and murmured something.

'What?' I said.

'Is there any water?'

I found the tumbler on the bedside table and turned back to the person beside me. She pushed herself up on one arm, took the glass with the other and drank, her head arched back and her neck exposed all the way down to the buttoned lace collar of her pink flannel nightdress.

A moment later, she had pulled the covers over her, rolled over to face away from me and was snoring quietly, the way she always used to.

In the morning, from the kitchen window, there is nothing to be seen but a white ground merging into the whitened sky. A granular, wind-sculpted bulk of snow covers the terrace, the wall, the woodpile, the outside table and chairs. Beyond that, nothing except teasing glimpses of our neighbour's vineyard, immediately whisked away by another flurry of snow swirled about by the wind gusting to and fro across the landscape beneath a high array of cloud.

Conditions on the roads are worse than I thought, and even with the Peugeot's four-wheel drive engaged we only just make it to the station in time. On the way, Claire explains the situation in a calm, no-big-deal tone to Daniel, who is wrapped up in his dressing gown and one of my father's padded jackets. The boy seems anxious and tearful, sensing that something important is happening which he doesn't understand. For the first time I begin to realize that this could turn out to be a complete disaster.

At the station, Claire finally manages to calm Daniel down enough to hand him over to me. At the east end of the stretch of straight track, the train appears in the distance.

'But what's going to happen?' I find myself asking in a panicky tone, almost as though I've been infected by Daniel's disease. 'Jean-Claude can't get a job in America, you can't work over here. Assuming this turns out to be serious, what are you going to do? How are you going to manage? Do you think it will all work out?'

She gives me another of those looks so expressive of the spaces and silences of this nubby new personality forged out of so much suffering. Comparing our respective losses for the first time, I am put to shame.

'I have absolutely no idea,' she says.

The train pulls in. When Claire climbs aboard, clutching her overnight bag, Daniel tries to follow. I hold him back, and he starts to scream and kick. The guard gives the signal and the train begins to move. Claire stands at a window, waving goodbye. Daniel looks after her, sobbing and protesting.

The drive back is a nightmare. I don't have a child seat, and Daniel refuses to stay put. In the end I turn round, drive into town and buy him a large ice-cream to keep him quiet until we get home. Up at the house, in the hills behind the coast, the weather has started to clear, with patches of blue sky opening up.

That's the extent of the good news, though. Daniel is still inconsolable at his mother's disappearance. I keep going over the story Claire and I agreed, about her going to see a friend for a few days and then coming back real soon with lots of presents. I might be speaking French for all the difference it makes.

But as Claire predicted, this fit soon passes. The next phase is an intensive search of every room in the house, just to make absolutely sure that this isn't some game, and that Mom isn't hiding somewhere, waiting to be discovered amid squeals of glee. Once this is over, he returns to the kitchen, an imposing figure in his tiny greatcoat.

'Not here,' he announces.

'She'll be back soon.'

But I know he's right. Lucy has left me for good.

The clockwork toys and pyromaniac stunts of the previous day no longer work their magic. They're associated with Mom's presence. I need to come up with something new. In the end, I take him to go and see Robert's chickens. We trudge across the snow-covered yard and up the steep flight of steps to the raised area above the house where the barn is located. I'm so busy making sure that Daniel is all right that I'm not looking where I'm going myself, and at the top of the steps I slip and land painfully on an outcrop of rock.

Daniel starts laughing loudly, his descant cackles rebounding from the rigid air. Adults don't fall over, he thinks, that's what toddlers do. So I must have done it deliberately, to entertain him, and he's determined to show his appreciation. I'm on my knees in a puddle of pink snow, my shin gashed open, and Daniel finally realizes that this is real, that I'm hurt. His laughter breaks off abruptly, and for a moment I'm worried that he's going to fall apart again. But he just comes to me, holding out his hand.

'Up again,' he says.

I know I should be reassuring him that everything's all right, that he needn't worry, but I can't. Instead I'm talking to someone I don't know who isn't even there. Thank you, I'm saying. Thank you for Lucy, thank you for Claire and for Daniel, thank you for this cold and this blood and this pain. Thank you. Thank you. Thank you.

ABOUT THE AUTHOR

Michael Dibdin is the author of thirteen previous novels. A native of England, he now lives in Seattle, Washington, with his wife, the mystery writer Katherine Beck.